Wildwitch

Wildfire

Lene Kaaberbøl

Illustrated by Rohan Eason

Translated by Charlotte Barslund

PUSHKIN CHILDREN'S BOOKS

Pushkin Press
71–75 Shelton Street
London, WC2H 9JQ

Wildwitch: Wildfire was originally published in
Danish as *Vildheks: Ildprøven* by Alvilda in 2010

This translation first published by Pushkin Children's Books in 2016

ISBN 978 1 782690 83 2

Set in Berling Nova by Tetragon, London
Printed and bound by CPI Group (UK) Ltd, Croydon CRO 4YY

www.pushkinpress.com

CONTENTS

1. Monster Cat   7
2. Cat Fever   13
3. Toad Venom and Snake Spittle   20
4. Blue Tits and Scarecrows   29
5. The Pencil Case Mouse   36
6. An Angel in the Mist   44
7. Self-defence for Wildwitches   54
8. Jumping Fleas   63
9. Wildways   75
10. Fire and Ashes   85
11. Blood and Red Rainbows   97
12. Purring Cats   103
13. The Coven Gathers   108
14. Raven Kettle   116
15. Tooth and Claw   128
16. To Run From a Fight   143
17. Skyfire   149
18. Waterfire   153
19. Earthfire   158
20. A Friend in Need   167
21. Heartfire   173
22. The Last Word   182

Wildwitch

Wildfire

CHAPTER 1

Monster Cat

The cat was standing on the stairs, refusing to budge.

It was the biggest cat I had ever seen. It was the size of my friend Oscar's labrador and just as black. Its eyes glowed neon yellow in the dim light of the stairwell that led up out of the bike basement.

"Ahem... hello, cat? Can I get past you, please?"

No.

Now I'm not saying that it actually spoke to me. But I could tell just by looking. It wasn't there by chance. This was no accident. It was there because it wanted to be there. Because it wanted something from me.

I was on my way to school and I was already late. It was wet and windy, which meant my bike ride wouldn't be very fast or much fun, either. And I didn't want to try and explain to Ruler-Rita, my scary Maths teacher, that I was late for her class for the second time in two weeks because I was too scared to take on a black cat.

"Shooooo," I hissed at it. "Go away! Beat it! Clear off!"

The cat merely opened its jaws to reveal a pink tongue and a set of white teeth longer and sharper than ordinary cats' teeth. And it was quite clearly better at hissing than I was.

I pushed my bike a little further up the ramp and moved up to the next step. The cat and I were now two metres apart. I flapped my hand at it.

"Go away!"

It didn't move an inch.

I know I'm not the bravest girl in the world, but at that moment I was more terrified of my Maths teacher than the cat. I took a deep breath and raced up the steps as fast as I could. The cat would have to get out of the way or...

The cat jumped. Not to the side or backwards, but right at me. It landed on my chest and face so that for a second all I could see was black fur. I stumbled back and fell down the stairs with my bike and the cat on top of me. My head slammed against the concrete floor and my elbow scraped the rough wall. But what really made me lie still, shocked and with my heart in my mouth, was the cat. Its yellow eyes burned into me, its claws dug through my raincoat, through my jumper, right through to my bare skin. It was a black, furry shape that almost filled my field of vision, and all I could see behind it was a leaden sky and the rain falling on us both in big, cold drops.

It held up its paw, then spread out and extended its claws. They were milky white with slate-grey tips.

"No," I pleaded. "Please don't..." Although I didn't know precisely what I was afraid it was going to do to me. My left arm was trapped under my body so I tried to push it away with my right hand. Its fur was wet and heavy, and not just from the rain. It smelled of seaweed, the sea itself and salt water. And I couldn't shift it at all.

Whoosh.

With one lightning-quick swipe its paw raked my face and I felt its claws rip the skin right between my eyes. The blood started flowing immediately, I could feel it trickling down the side of my nose and I had to blink to stop it running into my eyes. And while I lay there, stunned and bleeding, the monster cat leaned forwards and I felt the warm, rough rasp of its tongue against my forehead.

It was licking the blood from the cuts it had just inflicted on me.

"Clara! Do you know what time it is? You'll be late!" Mum called out from her study. I was standing in the hallway, unable to speak. A moment later she appeared.

"Little Mouse," she said and now she sounded frightened. "What happened?"

I shook my head. In fact I was shaking all over. My head hurt, the cuts to my forehead stung and burned, I thought I could still feel the weight of the cat's wet body on me and still smell seaweed and salty blood.

"A cat," I whispered. "There was... a cat."

I never thought for one minute that she would believe me. I expected her to ask me lots of questions and then accuse me of making it all up. I mean, how often do people get attacked by giant black cats?

But she didn't. She just stared at me.

"Oh, no," she said. That was all. And then she started to cry.

Perhaps I should explain a few things. My mum is no cry baby. Usually she's quite tough. She's a journalist and works freelance, that's what they call it when you work for yourself and you write articles for different newspapers that then pay you for them. And lots of newspapers do because she's a good reporter and she's clever at finding stories. My dad doesn't live with us and hasn't done since I was five, so Mum is used to handling most things on her own.

She soon stopped crying, found the first aid box and started cleaning the cuts to my forehead and my grazed elbow, her mobile wedged between her shoulder and ear while she tried to get through to the doctor.

"You are now number... seven... in the queue," said a tiny, remote, recorded voice. Mum pressed the "end call" button with an angry movement, then fetched a bag of frozen sweetcorn and a tea towel from the kitchen.

"Here you go," she said. "Press this against the cuts. I'm taking you to the doctor's."

"My bike," I said. "I haven't locked my bike."

"Don't worry about it," she said. "It doesn't matter. Go put on a dry top, we don't know how long we'll have to wait."

She was her old self again. My mum who always took charge, my mum who always looked after me. But I couldn't forget that helpless little "Oh, no." Or the look I had seen on her face before she put the mum-mask back on.

Her open mouth. Her lips that had gone all white. And the tears that had welled up in her eyes.

As if her whole world had just fallen apart.

CHAPTER 2

Cat Fever

"Take these for five days," the doctor said, handing my mum a prescription for penicillin. "And Clara... promise me you won't go teasing cats again."

"I didn't tease it," I protested. My head was still aching and it felt bigger and hotter than usual. My shoulder was sore from the tetanus injection, and the scratch marks on my forehead still stung and burned. It seemed so unfair that our usually friendly doctor was acting as if this were all my fault.

"No, no," she said. "But I suggest you keep away from cats for a while." She looked up at Mum again. "Call me if the cuts start to go red and swell up or if blisters begin to form. We don't want her getting Cat Scratch Disease."

"Cat Scratch Disease?" Mum said. "What's that?"

"Many cats carry a nasty bacterium called Bartonella. It can infect humans, but the penicillin should nip it in the bud, so there's nothing to worry about."

And I didn't or, at least, not much. I was much more scared that the monster cat might return.

On our way home we stopped at the chemist in Station Road and then at La Luna, our favourite pizza place.

"Hawaiian with extra cheese?" Mum asked me.

"Yes," I said, though it felt a bit weird to get a take-away for lunch. But the rain was still tipping down and my body felt heavy and flu-like. I didn't know if vast quantities of melted cheese would make me feel better, but it was definitely worth a try.

There was no question of my going to school that day. In fact, Mum acted as if it were only a matter of time before the Bartonella bacteria would wipe me out, despite the penicillin and the doctor's best efforts with iodine and surgical spirit. When we had finished the pizza and cleared the table, I wanted to go to my room and play on my computer, but Mum made me take a book and curl up under a blanket on the spare bed in her study while she worked. It was very cosy and I didn't mind, but I had a feeling that she was doing it to keep an eye on me.

Just after three o'clock that afternoon I got a text message. It was from Oscar. "Why weren't you at school today?" he wrote. I didn't know what to reply. It was a bit complicated to explain that I had been scratched by a cat and that it might make me ill. So I just texted back "sick :(", even though I wasn't really sick – at least, not yet.

That night I dreamt about the cat. It was waiting for me in the stairwell, just as it had done in real life. But instead of attacking me, it extended its body in a long, smug and supple cat-stretch, and yawned so I could see all its teeth. "You're mine now," it said, licking its lips with its pink tongue. "Mine, mine, mine..."

"Mum?"

"Yes, darling?" She sat up in bed with a start so fast that I wasn't sure she had even been asleep in the first place.

"Mum, I think I've got a temperature..."

My forehead was throbbing and my arms and

15

legs felt long and stiff, as if they weren't properly attached to my body. The light from Mum's bedside lamp drilled through my eyes and into my brain. I closed my eyes for a moment, but that was no good either because it made me so dizzy I could barely stand up straight.

Mum pulled me down onto the side of her bed and put her hand on my forehead.

"You're burning up," she said. "Does it hurt?"

"Yes."

"Lie down. I'll call the duty doctor."

The duty doctor, however, had no intention of making a house call just because some twelve-year-old girl had a bit of a temperature. I lay in Mum's bed with my eyes closed and heard her arguing with him. She sounded far away and strangely woolly even though she was sitting right next to me.

"But the penicillin isn't working, I've just told you," she said. "Her temperature is above forty degrees C!"

I started to drift off. There was a lovely clean and comforting smell of freshly-washed bed linen and of Mum and Mum's shampoo, but I was scared of falling asleep again. The cat was still there, I could feel it. It was waiting for me in my dreams.

"Would you like some water?"

"No, thanks." My throat was hot and raw and

I didn't want to swallow anything, even though I was actually quite thirsty.

"I think it's best if you drink something. A fizzy drink? Squash?"

"Some squash, please."

She fetched it for me. Then she went back into the kitchen and I heard her put the kettle on to make herself some coffee. She had taken her mobile with her and was calling someone.

"It's Milla Ash. I'm sorry to be calling you so late, but it's very important that I get hold of my sister..."

Then she closed the door and I couldn't hear the rest. But, despite the fever, I was intrigued. I knew that Mum had an older sister, but I'd never met her. And I couldn't even begin to imagine why Mum was trying to reach her at two o'clock in the morning. Perhaps she was a doctor? No, my Aunt Isa was an artist, I remembered. Once we had seen cards with very lifelike ducks on them in a shop window. *Isa Ash Design* it had said on a big sign, and the cards were really expensive. "She's called Ash, just like me," I had said, pointing at it. I wasn't very old then, eight or nine, I think. "That's because she's your aunt," Mum replied. But she didn't buy the cards and when I asked why we never visited Aunt Isa, Mum just muttered something about her living "miles away from anywhere", as if Aunt Isa lived in Outer Mongolia and we could only get there with a dog sled or by helicopter.

That was all I knew about my aunt. So why was it suddenly *very important* to get hold of her?

I closed my eyes, too tired to carry on thinking. But in the darkness behind my eyelids I could hear the cat singing: *Mine, mine, mine…* I opened my eyes again. I think I started to cry, mostly because I was exhausted, and yet I was too scared to go to sleep.

On the other side of the closed kitchen door, Mum's voice had grown loud and angry. I still couldn't make out every word she said, only something about *necessary* and *my daughter's life.*

My daughter's life? My heart skipped a beat. Did she think I was dying? Dangerous bacteria could kill you even if you weren't an oldie in a care home.

"Mum?" I called out. But she didn't hear me through the closed door. And anyway, she was probably too busy arguing on her mobile.

I sat upright. Bang! It felt as though I'd been whacked with a hammer right between the eyes, right where the cat scratches were. I whimpered. The pain was so intense, and it just wouldn't stop.

"Mum?"

I got out of bed. The door to the kitchen was miles away, but I reached it eventually.

"... I might just be forced to do that," Mum said. "But I simply don't understand how you can take that attitude when—"

Then she spotted me.

"Hello, Little Mouse. Sit down before you keel over." She turned away quickly, but I had seen it. She was crying. Again.

Mums aren't supposed to cry. They are supposed to be grown up and strong and take care of their kids. Like I said at the start, I'm not brave, not like Oscar, but I think that even Oscar would have been scared by now if he'd been in my place.

"Give me the address," Mum snapped. "And I'll work out the rest for myself." She scribbled furiously on the notepad on the fridge door and said a very curt goodbye to the person she was talking to. When she turned to face me again, she had wiped away her tears and was smiling in a very mum-like manner.

"Little Mouse, I think we have to go for a drive. Are you up to that?"

CHAPTER 3

Toad Venom and Snake Spittle

We drove for a long time. Mum had lined the backseat of our little blue Kia with pillows and duvets so I was really quite comfortable – apart from the fact that I was getting dizzier and there was a strange buzzing in my ears like an irritated mosquito, only louder and closer, as if it were actually inside my ear. *Mine, mine, mine.* I must have dozed off because when I woke up, we had left the city behind and there were no more street lights and no traffic noise around us, only darkness and the occasional headlights of another car. The windscreen wipers squealed across the windscreen, iiiiv-iiiiv-iiv, and the rain pelted onto the roof of the car.

"Please would you turn on the radio?" I asked, hoping it might drown out the mosquito sound.

"Yes, of course. Are you comfortable?"

"Fine," I said.

The speakers crackled while Mum tried to find a station with clear reception. Fragments of voices and music drifted past before breaking up into white noise.

"I don't think I can find a station this far out in the country," she said. "Why don't I put on a CD instead?"

"OK."

She found an Electra album which she knew I liked. Electra's clear, strong voice cut through the boom of the bass and the percussion beat. "Go where you gotta go, no matter how far," she sang. "Mamma always told me, gotta be who you are, can't be nobody else, gotta seek your own star, gotta be... gotta be... gotta be who you are."

I lay in the back, listening. My headache seemed to throb a little less violently when I concentrated on Electra rather than the mosquito. I braced myself.

"Mum?"

"Yes, Mouse?" She changed gear and accelerated. I could feel that we were driving uphill now.

"Is this... this disease. Is it something you can die from?"

She took her foot off the accelerator and the car slowed down almost immediately because the hill was so steep. Then she turned in her seat and looked at me.

"Clara Mouse. You mustn't think like that!" she exclaimed. "We're almost at Aunt Isa's and she'll help us. It's going to be all right. OK, sweetheart?"

"Yes," I mumbled. "OK."

But I said it mostly to humour her. As the car sped up again and we drove through the rain and the dark I could think of only one thing.

She hadn't said no.

The car rattled and shook as it went down a road so bumpy that Mum could only drive the Kia at a snail's pace. I decided to sit up. It was just too uncomfortable to be bounced around when I was lying down. I looked out between the front seats and tried to get a sense of where we were. The headlights swept across steep verges, puddles and tall, wet grass. The road had become almost a deep, wide hollow. The verges either side were higher than a person and, though it had stopped raining, I could see only a few stars because we were driving through a forest of giant, pitch-black spruces.

"Are we nearly there yet?" I asked.

"Nine minutes," Mum said. "Or at least that's what the sat nav is saying. I don't think it has factored in the state of this road." She tried to swerve around a hole, but the high verges made it impossible. Grrrrrrr. Something scraped against the bottom of the Kia. Perhaps travelling by helicopter or with huskies wouldn't have been such a bad idea after all.

It took more like twenty minutes before we turned right across a small wooden bridge and saw lights between the trees further ahead.

"This has to be the place," Mum said. "I can't imagine anyone else who would want to live so far away from civilization."

We drove through a gate and along a small field before Mum stopped the car in a yard between two buildings, a farmhouse and what looked to be some kind of stable. She parked next to an ancient Morris Minor with black side panels and a white roof. Both buildings had thatched roofs and thick stone walls. The light was on in the house and when Mum opened the car door I could smell wet soil, spruce and smoke from a log fire.

The entrance to the farmhouse was one of those doors that you sometimes see in stables. The top half was flung open and a tall, hunchbacked figure with long plaits appeared. No, wait. She wasn't a hunchback. The hump had feathers, eyes and wings. It was an owl and it was eyeing us as if we were something it might consider eating for its breakfast.

"Come in," said the strange lady with the owl. "And let me see what I can do."

This would appear to be my Aunt Isa.

Aunt Isa had lit a fire in the wood-burning stove of a large room which, to my eyes, was an odd mixture of workshop and lounge. A pot was bubbling away on the stove, regularly sending out small clouds of steam and acrid smells from under its lid. There were bookcases and cupboards along all available wall space, and the shelves held not only books, but also jars and glass containers, toolboxes and rows of baskets lined with newspaper. Later I learned that hibernating hedgehogs and dormice lived in some of them. There were a couple of non-matching armchairs, two long tables and a carpenter's work bench. The light was coming from two paraffin lamps. There was no sign of a TV.

I was lying on a faded old sofa that smelled of dog, with two patchwork quilts on top of my own duvet, and I was still freezing cold. Aunt Isa had been nice to me, but not quite so nice to my Mum, or so it seemed to me.

"Get some sleep if you can," Aunt Isa said to me. "You're safe here." Her eyes were the colour of autumn leaves and, for some reason, I believed her.

"The cat..." I whispered.

"Not here," she said. "It can only enter if I give it permission."

No further explanation was needed. She already knew. I had no idea how she could, but I was hugely relieved that she understood and didn't question me.

Towards Mum her voice was completely different – so sharp that you could cut yourself on it.

"You should have come much sooner."

"How could I?" Mum protested. "It only happened this morning."

"I know. But she turned twelve in March, didn't she?"

It wasn't exactly a difficult question, but Mum didn't reply. At first I thought she was just as confused as I was: I couldn't see what my birthday had to do with anything. But when she did say something, I could hear that she wasn't confused at all; she was angry and frightened.

"She's not like you," she said. "She's a sweet, bright and *normal* girl."

Aunt Isa looked long and hard at Mum. "Now is not the time to discuss that," she said. "First we need to get that fever down and get the child back on her feet."

Yes, please, I thought. And if you could make my headache go away while you're at it...

Aunt Isa lifted the lid and used a ladle to pour some of the pot's contents into a mug.

"Here," she said, handing me the mug. "It tastes a little bitter, but it'll do you good."

"What is it?" Mum asked, suspiciously.

"Toad venom and snake spittle," Aunt Isa said. "What did you think it was?"

I looked up, horrified, but then I saw the twinkle in her autumn-brown eyes.

"Don't worry," she said to reassure me. "I'm only teasing your mum. It's willow bark and herbs that will help the penicillin along. And when you've finished that, I'll massage your neck and your head. It all helps."

And it did. The toad venom – or whatever it was – tasted disgusting, to be honest, but when I'd drunk it, Aunt Isa sat down on the sofa with my head in her lap and started running her fingers firmly but gently up and down my throat, across my neck and all the way up to my hair. It felt soooooo nice. It was as if she took away a little bit of my headache with every stroke. Even when she started pressing the cuts on my forehead, which really were quite swollen, they didn't hurt at all.

She hummed while her fingers worked away, a wordless tune that rose and fell in strange rhythms; it wasn't a song I'd ever heard before. At times it sounded almost as if she were singing two notes at once, one low and one high. I don't know why, but it made me think of the wind and the rain and the smell of autumn leaves. Then without warning, I heard a door slam. I flung open my eyes, which, until then, had been well and truly shut.

"Mum?"

"She'll be back in a moment," Isa said. "She's not really into herbs and wildsong."

"Wildsong?"

"Hush. You think too much. We can talk about it later."

By now my headache had gone completely. And when I drifted off to sleep, there was no monster cat waiting for me in the shadows.

CHAPTER 4

Blue Tits and Scarecrows

When I woke up, my fever had gone. Breathing, however, was still difficult. Something heavy, warm and furry was lying across my chest, panting all over my face. When I opened my eyes, I found myself nose to nose with a huge, wrinkly-faced white and brown dog

"Hey," I whispered. "Sorry, but would you mind..."

Its tail thumped the duvet and I received an excited slobber on my cheek from a warm, pink tongue.

"Down, Bumble!" Aunt Isa ordered it.

Reluctantly, the dog shifted itself towards my feet.

"All the way down!"

The animal let out a deep, wet sigh and slid down onto the floor. I could breathe freely again.

"Sorry about that," Aunt Isa said. "Bumble's capacity for affection exceeds his intelligence. He has no sense of how large he actually is."

Bumble's tail was wagging so enthusiastically that Isa had to save a couple of cups from being swept off the coffee table. The dog was oblivious to her criticism. I couldn't help smiling and I soon discovered that Bumble had this effect on most people – or at least on anyone who didn't actually hate animals. He was so obviously just a big, happy and cuddly dog who loved everything and everybody, especially if they took the time to chat to him and scratch him behind his soft, brown ears.

"Is he a St Bernard?" I asked.

"I wouldn't know, you'd have to ask his parents," Isa said, unperturbed. "Some friends brought him to me. They found him with a broken front leg and he didn't have a microchip or a tattoo in his ear, so we couldn't work out where he came from. Now he lives here. And how are you feeling?"

"Good," I said, surprised to discover that it was actually true. I felt really quite good all over, I was no longer dizzy or sore and my headache had gone. "Where's my mum?"

"She's gone outside to see if she can get a signal on her mobile. You woke up a little earlier than we'd expected. Do you need the loo?"

I nodded. Suddenly I felt awkward being alone in a strange house with a woman I didn't know. All right, she was my aunt, but even so. And I was wearing my old Sesame Street pyjamas that I was too old and slightly too big for and my hair was a mess and I had four cat scratches between my eyes. What must she think?

But she didn't look as if she thought there was anything weird about it. Then again *she* was walking around with an owl on her shoulder... or that's to say...

"Where's the owl?"

"Hoot-Hoot? He's asleep in the barn. He's more sociable at night. Let me show you where the bathroom is."

In view of the stove, the paraffin lamps and the absence of a TV, I was half-expecting an earth closet or even a plank across a gully in the floor, like when Mum and I went on holiday to Turkey. Fortunately it turned out to be an ordinary loo, or

31

almost ordinary because to flush it I had to pull a handle at the end of a chain dangling from a cistern up on the wall, instead of pressing a button. Warm water came from a monster of a wall-mounted gas heater that was hissing away angrily between the sink and the bath tub.

I caught sight of myself in the mirror above the sink.

On a good day I would describe my hair as straight, soft and light brown and quite OK, really. My eyes are brown like Mum's – and just like Aunt Isa's, it occurred to me – and I have a sprinkling of freckles across my nose and cheeks, more in the summer than in the winter, but always a few. On a good day I can almost convince myself that I look cute in my own special way, though I'm not exactly model gorgeous.

Today was not one of those days.

My hair was limp and wispy and a very dull shade of brown, I was so pale that my freckles looked like fly droppings and, though my forehead was no longer swollen, I still had four deep, red scratches between my eyes, which somehow managed to make me look really bad-tempered.

"I hope they'll go away," I muttered to myself and touched them very carefully.

"Tweeeet?" something said. I spun around. On the windowsill, in a small cardboard box that said *Wendleham's Lavender Soap* on it, a blue tit was watching me through its small, shiny, black eyes. It tilted its head and tweeted again. Then it opened its beak in expectation and rocked from side to side as if waiting for me to feed it.

"I'm not your mum," I told it.

"Tweeeeeeeet!"

"Stop it. I don't even know what someone like you eats."

"Tweeeeet!!!" The blue tit was quite insistent now.

"Don't let her boss you around," said Aunt Isa from the doorway. "I nursed her when she broke her wing last summer, but it healed long ago and she's perfectly capable of looking after herself. It's just that she likes the service here." She opened the bathroom window and tapped the soapbox with her finger.

"Come on. Get off your backside," she ordered it. "There's a feed ball hanging from the apple tree!"

"Tweeet..." Sulking, the blue tit flapped out of the open window.

Mum smelled of spruce trees and morning dew when she came back. But she didn't look happy and, when she went to pack the car, she was really quick about it so that we could leave straight after breakfast.

"I'm glad you're better, sweetheart," she said. And there was no doubt that she was happy and relieved, but even so I could feel that something still wasn't quite right.

"What is it?" I asked.

"Nothing, Mouse. Have you cleaned your teeth?"

"Yes. Mum, what is it?"

She shook her head. "I'm just a bit stressed. It's been a busy week."

Now that might be one reason, but something was definitely wrong between her and Aunt Isa.

"I hope you know what you're doing," Isa said.

"I do," Mum said sharply. "I've got my life and you've got yours."

"Yes," Aunt Isa said. "But what about Clara?"

"Thank you for helping her," Mum said. "But it's time for us to go now."

And fifteen minutes later we were back in the car, me in my pyjamas and a grey woolly jumper that Isa had lent me, Mum wearing the same clothes she had put on when I woke her up in the

34

middle of the night. We looked like a pair of tired scarecrows. But Mum was obviously in a hurry to get home. The Kia rattled down the gravel road as fast as it could. Behind us, Isa and Bumble stood in the yard, waving. Or rather Isa waved. Bumble wagged his tail.

We turned into the wood and I lost sight of them. I was surprised to discover that it made me sad. Strange, really, since I had been with them for less than twelve hours, and slept for most of it. But that was how it was – as if I were already missing them.

"Please could we visit Aunt Isa another time?" I said. "And maybe stay a bit longer?"

"Perhaps," Mum said. But she said it in that special Mum-voice that really meant no.

CHAPTER 5

The Pencil Case Mouse

"What happened to you?"

Oscar pointed an accusatory finger at me as if it were completely unacceptable that I had had an adventure without him. Or rather, he wasn't pointing at me, but at the cat scratches on my forehead. Though almost a week had passed, they were still an angry red and very noticeable, and today was the first day Mum thought I was well enough to go back to school.

"I was attacked by a cat," I said. "And I don't want to talk about it."

He was about to laugh, I could see that, but he stopped himself.

"Are you OK?" he asked, very serious now.

Did I really look that bad? I no longer had a temperature, but I still had trouble sleeping.

"I don't know really," I said. "At first I got sick

as a dog... but then... I got better." I wanted to tell him about Aunt Isa, but for some reason I held back. Usually we tell each other everything. Oscar is my best friend. We've known each other since we were in nappies and we actually mingled our blood once to seal our friendship after we had read in a book about taking blood oaths – we were quite young at the time, and I guess we thought it sounded cool. Sometimes the others tease us and say we're snogging, even though we're not. Oscar goes red all over and has even got into fights over it a couple of times, but he carries on being my friend.

He bit his lip. I don't think he quite knew what to say. His blond, spiky hair stuck out as usual, and there's something about his cheeks and mouth that always makes him look as if he's about to burst out laughing. But he looked worried.

"Do you want me to carry your bag?" he asked, which was incredibly sweet of him, especially because it was guaranteed to make the others start chanting: *Clara and Oscar sitting in a tree*, k I s s I n g.

"Thanks," I said. "But I can manage. I'm OK, really. I'm just not sleeping very well at the moment."

In Literacy we were doing project work, which meant we were split into groups of four to look for adjectives in one chapter of a book we were reading. I was in a group with Josefine, who can be really hard work. She always wants to be in charge and she immediately divided the chapter into four sections, then told everyone to go through whichever section she gave us, rather than talk about everything as a group.

No one really tried to object. Least of all me. I'm not someone who speaks up in class and Josefine has a knack of making me feel even smaller and stupider than usual. And while she was making notes in her exercise book, she also appeared to be keeping an eye on me.

"Clara, 'accidentally' is not an adjective! If you don't know what you're doing then why don't you ask?"

"Why can't we work together?" I said, well aware that my cheeks had gone red with embarrassment.

"It's much faster if we do it my way," she said and she was probably right, but it wasn't much fun.

At least not until Josefine let out a bloodcurdling scream and jumped away from the table.

"Mouuuuse!" she squealed, pointing a quivering finger at me. "Mouuuuuuuuuuuuuuse!"

I'm not exaggerating. Her squeal lasted several seconds.

And she was right. On the table in front of me, in my open pencil case, there was a skinny, grey mouse. But not for very long, because, halfway through Josefine's scream, it darted across the table and hopped inside my left sleeve.

"Josefine, stop screaming," said Erik, our teacher. "What mouse?"

"There," she said, flapping her hands in my direction. "In Clara's pencil case!"

"I can't see a mouse."

"No, not now, but..."

"Did anyone else see it?" Erik asked. Marcus and Tea, the two other members of our group, shook their heads. Because Josefine had been screaming, they had been looking at her and not at the mouse.

I said nothing. I could feel the mouse's small, warm body on my forearm, under my sleeve, I could feel its small, prickly claws and the soft fur on its belly, but I still said nothing.

"There *was* a mouse," Josefine insisted.

Erik bent down and looked under the table. Everyone else in the classroom promptly copied him and looked at the floor and under the chairs and tables, too.

"Oh look, a mouuuuse!" Amjad whined in a shrill voice that was meant to make fun of Josefine, and most of the others started to laugh.

"Yes, all right, that's enough, Amjad. Everyone sit down again. Josefine, if there was a mouse, at least it's gone now. Back to work!"

For the rest of the lesson I sat very still with the mouse hidden up my sleeve and found it hard to concentrate on the difference between adjectives and adverbs. The mouse did nothing. It didn't move except for a faint quiver every now and then. It didn't try to run further up my arm and it had obviously decided it was unwise to try and stick its nose out again. So it stayed put – and waited. Without knowing why, I let it do that. And when the lesson finally ended, I packed up my books without using my left arm too much, slung my backpack over my shoulder, took my jacket from the row of pegs and left.

"Aren't you going to put on your jacket?" Oscar asked. "I mean, you've just been ill..."

It sounded strangely mummyish coming from him, but I actually think he was a little worried about me. I glanced around. Josefine wasn't nearby and Erik was some distance away, talking to another teacher.

"I've got a mouse up my sleeve," I whispered.

"What?"

"Shhhh."

He stared at me. "Is it tame?" he said. "Is it one of those white ones?"

"No. Come with me. I have to find out what it wants."

"What are you talking about?"

As I uttered those words, I could hear how crazy they sounded. But I just knew that the mouse wanted something. It was no coincidence that it had hidden itself first in my pencil case and now up my sleeve.

"I know it sounds weird," I said.

He laughed. "Hey. You *are* weird," he said. "Nothing new there then."

"No, I'm not. I'm completely normal." Small, shy and plain, perhaps, but definitely normal. Or

I was until a giant cat attacked me and made me look like I'd picked a fight with a garden rake. "I'm no weirder than you!"

"Come on," was all he said. "I want to see that mouse."

We went to the old toilets in the school playground, which hardly anyone ever used because they stank and were built in the days when children wore short trousers and got caned regularly. Carefully, I pulled up my sleeve so that we could both see the mouse.

It was an ordinary house mouse with grey fur and a long nose, white whiskers and shiny black eyes. Its front paws were pink and looked like tiny hands. It didn't run away, no, it sat up on its hind legs and wrinkled its nose.

"It's very sweet," Oscar said. "But it has to be someone's pet, it's completely tame."

"I don't think so," I said.

"Why not? A wild mouse would have run away ages ago."

"Something's wrong with it," I said. "Look at its nose."

Oscar bent down to get a better look. "Yes," he said. "It's hurt itself."

I gently raised my arm until I held the mouse at eye-level. It went down on all fours to get a slightly better grip with its pink paws, but otherwise it stayed where it was.

Oscar was right. On one side of its nose there was a clot of dried blood and pus, and something black was sticking out from the centre of it. A thorn. A thin thorn from a bush had pierced the mouse's upper lip and got stuck so the mouse couldn't close its mouth properly.

"Oh, you poor mouse," I whispered. "That's why you're so thin. You can't eat." And without even thinking about it, I pinched the thorn with my thumb and index fingernails, and pulled it out.

The mouse emitted a small, shrill squeak and rubbed its nose with its front paws ten or twelve times. Then it darted along my arm, across my stomach and down my trouser leg until it could jump safely onto the old, red floor tiles. There it squatted on its hind legs for a brief second and rubbed its nose again. It looked almost as if it were waving.

"Goodbye," I said. "Take care!"

A quick movement, little more than a grey flash, and it was gone. It disappeared with familiar ease into the crack between the threshold and the floor. Oscar stared after it. Then he looked hard at me.

"OK," he said. "So you still think you're normal? You can forget about that."

CHAPTER 6

An Angel in the Mist

We cycled home from school together, Oscar and I. We both live in Jupiter Crescent, only he lives in the block that faces Jupiter Avenue, whereas Mum and I live in the one overlooking Mercury Street. They're old buildings with high ceilings and tiny bathrooms. There's a green area inside the courtyard with trees and bushes like chestnuts and lilacs, and it's so overgrown that it's like a wonderful jungle. According to Mum, my friendship with Oscar began when we were sat at opposite ends of the sandpit in the courtyard, took one look at each other and then crawled towards the other as fast as we could, spraying sand and knocking over plastic buckets and other kids in the process. Oscar's mum is a single parent, too. Her name is Marlena and she is a lawyer in an office somewhere in the city.

We were able to ride our bikes next to each other on the cycle path for most of the journey. The weather was grey and foggy, and water splashed everywhere when we rode our bikes through the puddles. The cycle path ended when we reached Station Road, so I had to pull in behind Oscar and cycle single-file. Cars rushed past us and sprayed our legs.

"Very foggy, isn't it?" Oscar called over his shoulder, slowing down.

And it was. The tarmac was shiny and wet. A clammy, grey mist lingered between the houses. It was so dense that the street lamps had come on though it was only two in the afternoon.

"We'd better get off and push," I said. "It's really hard to see where we're going."

We jumped off our bikes and pushed them on the pavement down the last stretch of Station Road.

"I can barely make out the traffic lights," Oscar said.

And he was right. We had to squint to see whether the man at the pedestrian crossing was red; all we could make out was a faint red glow in the fog. When it changed to green, we started crossing. And then something really weird happened.

The pavement disappeared.

I know it sounds crazy. But when we reached the other side of the street, there was no pavement. Instead of paving stones and cobbles there was grass. Dense grass, ankle-high, like a lawn that hasn't been cut for weeks.

I stopped.

"Oscar..."

"Yes?" he said.

"Where has the pavement gone?"

He didn't say anything for a while. We both stood there and I couldn't see anyone but him and me, our bikes – and then the grass, which shouldn't have been there at all.

"Perhaps we wandered into someone's garden by accident," Oscar suggested.

"In Station Road? There aren't any gardens."

"Then we must be lost, I guess..."

The fog moved around us in slow, grey spirals. We couldn't even see the house wall, though we must be standing right next to it. The traffic noise had faded away. And we could no longer see people, cars or bikes moving in the fog. I felt a strange, wet prickling at the back of my neck – as if a ghost were standing behind me, tapping my shoulder. I spun around. There was only more fog.

Suddenly a gust of wind swept the fog away. Or, at least, some of it. A kind of tunnel was created down the middle, a grass tunnel whose ceiling and walls were made of fog. And down this path something was coming towards me.

It wasn't a human being. I've certainly never seen a human being with wings reaching a couple of metres above their head. It made her look enormous even though without the wings she was only slightly taller than me. And she hadn't even unfurled them. They were closed and they weren't white as I thought they would be, but brown and grey like the wings of a bird of prey.

Her face was also narrow and birdlike, with a pointy chin and a sharp nose that stuck out almost like a beak. And her eyes flashed yellow. I know this because she was looking straight at me.

"Witch child," she said in a hissing, lisping voice. "Blood of Viridian. Come with me."

I took a step forward without giving it a second thought. When an angel calls you, you come. And she had to be an angel, didn't she? She had wings.

Then two things happened in quick succession. Something struck the side of my thigh and I stumbled. Then a black shadow charged at the angel with a wild and piercing war cry, and I recognized the distinctive wet seaweed smell of the giant cat. The angel retreated a few steps and raised her hands – except they looked more

like claws because her nails were twice as long as her fingers. The cat pounced on her. They both screamed, each as high-pitched as the other, and a thin fountain of blood spurted up into the air and turned into a spray of tiny, red droplets.

At the same time Oscar grabbed me and pulled me aside so we both fell over and landed in a jumble of bike wheels, arms and legs.

"Look out!" he shouted.

A lorry appeared out of the fog. Headlights, squealing brakes, the roar of a diesel engine and a radiator grille, everything came thundering right at us and I yelped, a feeble, terrified squeak, and rolled out of the way as fast as I could.

There was a crunching sound and a strong smell of burnt rubber.

I lay on the pavement with my back pressed up against a wall with Oscar sprawled across my legs. The radiator grille of the lorry loomed large a very short distance from us and both our bikes lay crushed under its massive front wheels.

The door to the driver's cabin was opened and the driver jumped out. His face was deathly pale under the shade of his trucker's cap.

"What happened?" he said. "Are you OK? I didn't see you because of the fog, not until the last minute. Please tell me that you're all right."

The angel had gone. The cat had gone. There was no longer a tunnel through the fog, and the fog itself was lifting.

I shifted, mostly to make sure that I still had my arms and legs and could move them. I could. But Oscar lay still.

"Oscar?" I whispered. And then much louder: "Oscar!"

"All right, all right," he grunted irritably, as if I'd told him to wake up and go to school. "Ouch. Ouch, my head hurts."

He half sat up and I saw a thin line of blood trickle from a cut to his forehead. He must have bashed his head against either the wall or the pavement. But at least he was able to sit up, look at me and speak.

By now several onlookers had gathered. One of them, an elderly lady in a shaggy green winter coat, had already got her mobile out and was making a call.

"Hello? Emergency services? We need an ambulance for the corner of Station Road and West Street. There's been an accident..."

Oscar was admitted to hospital for "observation for concussion". Fortunately, I was allowed to go home. I had a fresh graze to my elbow, almost on top of the one I got when I tumbled down the stairwell with the cat. I wasn't concussed, but it felt as if everything inside me had been shaken up.

I had seen an angel. And I had come very close to dying. Were the two things connected? Had the angel come to fetch me when the cat attacked her? And what was it she'd called me? Witch child. And something to do with blood?

To an outsider it was straightforward: a couple of kids on their way home from school stray onto the road in the fog. A lorry driver slams on the brakes just in time, luckily. The boy hits his head, the girl is unharmed. End of story.

But that was only the half of it. The angel, the cat and the pavement that turned into grass... the police report made no mention of them because I was apparently the only one who had seen them. Not even Oscar. He had seen the grass, that was something at least. But not the angel or the cat. How could he not have seen something that was almost four metres tall? It was beyond me.

Mum rang up Marlena, Oscar's mum, and learned that the hospital would keep him overnight, but that he was fine and would probably be discharged in a day or two.

"He saved my life," I said. It sounded dramatic to say it out loud, but it was the truth. If he hadn't pulled me aside, the lorry would have run me over. And then the angel would probably have taken my soul or whatever it was she had come for.

"You *have* to look where you're going," Mum said, and started shouting at me again because she was so upset. "It's not as if you don't know how to handle yourself in traffic!"

"Mum..."

"Yes. Sorry, Clara Mouse. I know it was foggy. But you *have* to look..."

It was the tenth time she'd said it, at least. I was so tired that I began to cry and I blinked to make the tears go away, but they refused.

"I was looking! It wasn't my fault!" I couldn't bear her telling me off any longer. Not now. "Something's wrong. There's something wrong with me, isn't there? She called me a witch child..."

Mum froze. She was still holding the mobile in her hand.

"Who did?" she said.

"Her. The angel. But I was the only one who saw her, Oscar didn't. And he didn't see the cat either..."

And it all poured out of me, the tunnel in the fog, the pavement that turned into grass, the giant wings and the hissing voice, the cat's war cry and the smell of seaweed.

Mum listened without interrupting. She sat down at the kitchen table next to me and took in everything I told her without saying a single word. It wasn't until I got to the bit about the ambulance taking Oscar away and the bikes that were squashed and bent that she put her arm around me, held me close and murmured into my hair.

"We have to do it."

"Do what?" I said.

"You and I are going on a little holiday. To your Aunt Isa."

CHAPTER 7

Self-defence for Wildwitches

"It's not all that big," Aunt Isa said. "But if we tidy up, I'm sure it'll be fine."

She looked around the attic room as if she expected the trunks, boxes and piles of clothes to just get up and march out the door of their own accord.

"I can do that," Mum offered. "Just tell me where to put stuff."

"Most of it can go in the loft in the stable," Aunt Isa said.

"Can't I just sleep on the sofa like I did last time?" I protested.

"That's where Bumble sleeps." Aunt Isa lifted a dusty removal crate from the old iron bedstead that was standing under the sloping ceiling. "You ought to have your own room."

It sounded so... permanent. As if I were going

to live here and not just have "a little holiday", as Mum had called it.

Two weeks ago I hadn't even met my Aunt Isa. Now I was about to get my own room in her house. I'd sussed that it had something to do with these strange events – the cat, the angel and the fog. But what was it really all about?

"Could somebody please tell me what's going on?" I pleaded.

Mum and Isa looked at each other. Then Mum nodded, slowly and reluctantly.

"Please would you do it?" she asked Isa. "You're better at it than I am." And then she looked away as if she were ashamed. Aunt Isa knitted her brows.

She began, "How long were you planning to avoid—" but then she interrupted herself. "No. We can discuss that later. Come on, Clara. I'll make us a cup of tea and then try to answer your questions."

So while Mum scrambled about in the attic and made it habitable, Aunt Isa and I sat at a small table with a gingham tablecloth in the corner of the kitchen and drank tea. Bumble forced himself under the table between our legs though there was barely room for him. On the windowsill by the sink a blackbird was nestled in a shoebox full of shredded newspaper. It watched us with black beady eyes while calmly preening its wing.

"So what do you want to know?" Aunt Isa said.

About a million things, I thought. But which one was the most important?

"Am I going to die?" I burst out before I had decided whether I wanted to say it out loud.

Aunt Isa's eyebrows shot up and several lines appeared across her forehead.

"Why do you think that?" she said.

"Because... first there was the cat and the bacteria that can kill you... and then... yesterday... that angel came to fetch me. And Oscar and I nearly got run over by a lorry."

Isa put down her mug. "What did the angel look like?" she asked.

I tried to describe her.

"Big," I said. "Or rather her wings were big. Enormous. And they weren't white, sort of mottled grey and brown. She had yellow eyes. I didn't think angels would have eyes like that."

Isa closed her eyes for a moment. When she opened them again, she looked at me for a long time. For so long that I started to feel very uncomfortable.

"That was no angel," she said at last.

"Then what was it?"

"Once she was a wildwitch. What she is now... I don't think even she can answer that."

The flame in the paraffin lamp didn't flicker, nor did an icy chill pass through the room. But it felt as if the kitchen had suddenly turned darker and colder.

"Who is she?" I asked in a voice that sounded smaller than normal.

"She calls herself Chimera. Never speak her name anywhere but in this house, it's already too easy for her to find you."

"Find me? What does she want with me?"

Isa reached out her hand and stroked my cheek lightly. "I don't know, Clara. But we have to make sure that she doesn't get you."

Aunt Isa told me to put on my coat and boots, and we went outside. We walked down the gravel road and crossed the small field with the brook in it before we reached the gate.

"This far," she said, pointing at three white stones dug into the ground so that I could only just make them out. "You must never go further than here unless I'm with you."

"Why?" I asked.

"Because I can't protect you if you go beyond my wildward."

"What—?"

"—is a wildward? An area protected by a wild-witch."

It was the second time she'd mentioned that word. Wildwitch. I looked at my aunt in the twilight. Hoot-Hoot had come flying the moment we stepped outside and had settled on her shoulder. Aunt Isa was wearing an ordinary raincoat and an old yellow rain hat, and she had stuffed her brown plaits inside the collar so I couldn't see them.

"You're a witch," I said. And it wasn't a question.

"A wildwitch," she said, as if it were the most natural thing in the world. "I take care of everything that lives in the wild, and in return they look after me." Bumble wagged his tail and Hoot-Hoot rubbed his beak against the brim of her yellow hat.

"But you said that Chimera is a wildwitch, too..."

"No. I said that she *used* to be one. She broke her witch's oath a long time ago, and now she takes whatever she wants without giving anything back."

I remembered the angel creature. Her yellow eyes, her sharp face. *Come with me, witch child.*

"Why... does she want *me*?"

Isa shook her head. "I don't know, Clara."

"She called me a witch child," I said. "But Mum... my mum is no witch."

"No. Your mum desperately wants everything to be ordinary and normal, to live in a world where what you see is what you get. But the world isn't like that." Isa tilted her head slightly and looked at me; she narrowed her eyes a little. I could feel her gaze. It was as if she had pointed a torch at my face. "Clara... would you be very upset if I told you that I think you're a wildwitch – or that you could be one, if you wanted to?"

Hoot-Hoot flapped his wings without making a noise. They were pale on the underside, almost silver, and I looked at him and his silver wings so that I wouldn't have to look at my aunt.

"But I don't know what that means," I said at length. "Will I have to live in a cave in the forest, can I ever have any friends...?"

"Of course you can have friends," Isa said. "Only some of them will have feathers or fur."

I shook my head. "It's not that I don't like animals..."

" – but you'd also like to have some friends who don't poo on the floor and regularly regurgitate mouse bones? Don't worry, you'll meet people as well. Perhaps as soon as tomorrow. Clara, you don't have to live like I do or be anything like me. But you will have to learn enough so that you can at least take care of yourself."

"How do I do that?"

"We'll make a start on that tomorrow. Self-defence for wildwitches, lesson one."

When we got back, Mum had finished clearing out the attic room. She had lit a paraffin lamp and made the bed with several duvets and pillows and a faded old black-and-white-chequered quilt with tiny red rosebuds embroidered on every single square. The sloping ceiling, the little round window and the pink rag rug on the floor made the room look really quite cosy. But there was only one bed in it.

"Where are you going to sleep?" I asked her.

Mum sat down on the bed and patted the quilt.

"Clara Mouse. Sit down for a moment."

She said it in her we-need-to-talk-about-something voice and the knot in my stomach, which had been there ever since the day Oscar and I nearly got run over, grew bigger.

"What is it?" I said.

"I have to go back to town."

The knot now filled my whole stomach. It pushed upwards and squashed my heart. It pushed downwards and made me feel like I needed to pee.

"But you can't," I whispered. Somehow this was worse than all the other things put together. That

I might be a wildwitch like Aunt Isa. That I had nearly died – twice – in just over a week, that a monster cat was persecuting me, that a non-angel was chasing me and scaring even Aunt Isa – I might be able to cope with all that as long as my mum was with me.

"I have to," she said.

"Can't you just work here? There has to be somewhere nearby where you can get Wi-Fi..."

"It's not work, Clara. How could you think that? You're far more important than my stupid work." She looked grim and miserable.

"Then what is it?"

She made no reply. She just put her arm around my shoulder and gave me a little squeeze.

"Clara, we have no choice," she said. "I agree that it's awful. I'm the one who should be looking after you, not Isa. But I can't protect you, not against all this. I can't do what she can."

"But how long will I have to stay here?"

"Until Isa says it's safe for you to come home."

Probably when I had passed *Self-defence for wildwitches, lesson one*. Whatever that was.

"But what if I don't want to?"

"Clara Mouse. You have to. Listen to me. You have to promise me that you'll do everything Aunt Isa tells you. If... if there were any other way, do you think I would ever leave you here? And you won't be here very long."

"How long?"

"A few weeks, perhaps. If you work really hard."

"And then everything will be like it was before? And I can come home again?"

"Yes."

A couple of weeks. I suppose I could manage that.

"OK," I said. "I'll do it."

"I'm glad, Little Mouse." She kissed my hair.

Mum left shortly after we'd eaten. That night I slept for the first time in the attic room under the sloping ceiling, with the wind singing in the trees outside and the rain lashing the little, round window.

CHAPTER 8

Jumping Fleas

I woke up with a disorienting feeling of having dreamt bizarre and crazy dreams all night. The room was cold, much colder than my bedroom at home, which had a radiator. The thought of leaving my warm nest of duvets and extra quilts wasn't very appealing, but I needed to pee and my tummy was rumbling with hunger. I reached out for my sweater and jeans and got dressed under the duvets. Then I got up.

When I reached the stairs, I heard voices coming from the kitchen. I got very excited because I thought at first that Mum had come back, but then I realized I didn't recognize the second voice, it was lighter and younger than Mum's, and had an accent that sounded foreign.

"How long will she be here?"

"I don't know, Kahla," Aunt Isa replied. "It depends on how quickly she learns."

"Then I hope she's a fast learner. And that she doesn't scare so easily that she wets herself every time she meets anything bigger than a house mouse."

"Kahla!"

"I'm just telling it like it is."

"No. You're telling it as you think it is. And if you want to be a proper wildwitch you have a lot to learn about compassion and good manners!"

I was now outside the kitchen door and felt no urge to go in. She hated me. Whoever Kahla was. She hadn't even met me yet and already she had made up her mind that she didn't like me, and she clearly thought that I was going to be hopeless and stupid and ridiculous.

I knew I shouldn't care about it. Or perhaps I should get mad. But that's not how I am. When people think mean things about me, then I become hopeless and stupid and ridiculous, and I can't make head or tail of anything. I couldn't even open the kitchen door.

"Clara?" Aunt Isa said suddenly. "Why don't you come in?"

She couldn't see me, but perhaps she'd heard me. At any rate she knew that I was there. I pushed open the door. I was glad that I'd got dressed. It was bad enough that my hair was sticking out to all sides, but at least I wasn't wearing my too-short Sesame Street pyjamas and my feet weren't freezing cold.

"Hi," I said.

Bumble's tail bashed the floor cheerfully, thump-thump-thump, but it seemed to be too early in the morning for him to bother getting up. Isa smiled when she saw me. And a girl who had to be Kahla sent me the darkest, surliest look anyone had shot me for a long time. She was practically giving me the finger.

"Good morning, Clara. Kahla, this is Clara, my niece. And Clara, this is Kahlamindra Millaconda, who is also my student."

She wasn't very tall, but she was round like a snowman. Not necessarily because she was fat, but because she was wrapped in so many layers of clothing that she looked like she would roll if you knocked her over. Even indoors she was wearing a woolly hat, one of those Inca-style knitted ones with ear flaps and a small pom-pom on top, as well as countless scarves, thick woolly jumpers, vests, felted boots, trousers and woolly skirts in all the colours of the rainbow plus one or two the rainbow had never heard of. Pitch-black hair stuck out from under her Inca hat, and what little of her skin wasn't covered by three layers of coloured wool had a warm cinnamon glow.

"Hi," I mumbled.

"Hi," she said.

And that was all we could think of saying to each other. If Aunt Isa had had Kahla in mind when she talked about my making friends who didn't regularly regurgitate mouse bones... well, it looked like I'd be in for a long wait.

We ate breakfast in a strained silence while we sized each other up across the porridge bowls. Aunt Isa looked at us in turn, but made no attempt to break the ice and get Kahla and me to talk to each other, which I was grateful for. When we'd put our bowls and the pot in the sink to soak, Aunt Isa took us both outside. It was a cold November day and the rain was spitting. We followed her up the hill behind the stable, Kahla and I, and Bumble, obviously, who kept wagging his tail and clearly thought the whole thing was an awfully big adventure. I was a lot less enthusiastic. The ground was wet and slimy and I slipped quite a few times, once so badly that I ended up with muddy brown patches on the knees of my trousers. I glanced furtively at Kahla. She skipped up the path with ease and agility despite her many layers. I wouldn't have believed it was humanly possible to wear more items of clothing than she already was, but she had managed to add a pink quilted jacket and a red scarf, plus a stripy scarf tied around her Inca hat, plus a pair of bright yellow mittens with red hearts – and even so she could still walk. It was nothing short of a miracle.

Aunt Isa stopped halfway up the hill and pointed to a messy pile of twigs and rotting leaves.

"Can either of you tell me what happened here?" she said.

"A dog or a fox has been digging for something," Kahla said immediately. She bent over and studied the ground. "Not a fox," she then said. "The paw prints are too big. The dog probably scented the hedgehog and dug it out. Now the hedgehog's winter hideaway has been destroyed. Stupid dog."

Bumble looked nervous.

"Not you," she said, stroking his head with her mitten hand. "You would never do a thing like that, would you?"

How could she see all that? It was just a pile of twigs and a hollow with a bit of withered grass in it. When I looked hard, I could see some scratches where the dog had been digging, but how could she know the rest?

"That's right," Aunt Isa said. "Well spotted, Kahla. Now can you find the hedgehog?"

Kahla closed her eyes for a moment. She started humming faintly, a wordless song that bounced back and forth between two tones, one high and one low. It reminded me of the time Aunt Isa had made my headache go away. Kahla turned slowly on the spot as if she were a radar scanner, and then suddenly pointed down the hill, slightly to the right of the stable.

"That way," she said. "It's not very far, only twenty or thirty paces." She started walking, diagonally through bushes and scrub. Aunt Isa and I followed, zigzagging to avoid the worst obstacles.

And there really was a hedgehog exactly where she'd said it would be. It had curled up under a thorn bush, but even I could see that this wasn't a very good choice of hideout. This was no warm, dry nest of grass, and the branches of the bush were nothing like the dense cover that the twigs had provided.

"It can't survive here," Kahla said quietly. "Do you want us to bring it back to the house?"

"Yes," Aunt Isa said. "But first we have to solve a small problem."

"And what's that?" Kahla asked.

Isa smiled.

"A flea hunt," she said. "It's today's lesson."

At first Kahla looked incredulous. Then her dark eyes flashed with anger.

"Fleas?" she said. "You want us to waste time on fleas?"

Isa nodded, taking no notice of Kahla's outraged face.

"Fleas are a part of the natural world," she said. "But that doesn't mean that I want them inside my house." She took a white tea towel from her basket and spread it on the ground. She carefully picked up the hedgehog and placed the small animal in the middle of it. She closed her eyes for a moment and hummed a few notes. At first I didn't really think that anything was happening, but then I saw them: ten or twelve tiny black dots appeared on the white fabric around the hedgehog. And, as I kept watching, another four or five fleas jumped from the body of the hedgehog and onto the tea towel.

Aunt Isa lifted the hedgehog into the basket.

"Your turn," she said. "Kahla, you go first. You call the fleas on the left half of the tea towel. And only those!"

Kahla rubbed her nose with her mitten. "Can't I just call them all?"

"No. This task is about precision. Off you go."

Kahla didn't seem to need any instructions. Just like my aunt had, she closed her eyes for a moment. Then she started humming.

Soon the fleas were no longer scattered across the tea towel in a random pattern. A tight little formation of flea soldiers lined up on an area the size of a thumbnail, and started marching towards the edge of the tea towel in regular little jumps.

I stared. I blinked. And I stared again.

But no matter how many times I blinked, the fleas kept marching in unison. In ruler-straight lines.

"Stop," Isa said.

Kahla opened her eyes. "What?" she said. "Why?"

"You've rounded them all up. I only wanted half, thank you."

Kahla frowned. "But they're so small," she said, sounding frustrated. "I can't tell them apart!"

"Try."

Kahla was clearly annoyed at the criticism, but she didn't say anything. She rubbed her nose again, the formation fell apart and the fleas scattered across the tea towel once more. She closed her eyes. Hummed a couple of notes – more quietly this time, but the same tune. As before, the fleas lined up in formation. Kahla clenched her fists and bit her lip. She suddenly seemed out of breath. But then one black dot separated from the troop and jumped towards the edge of the tea towel. It was followed by another and another until exactly nine out of eighteen fleas had disappeared into the forest floor.

"Excellent," Isa praised her. "I told you you could do it."

Kahla's frozen face lit up in a smile, the first I had seen from her all morning. Her dark eyes beamed.

"I did it!" she said. "I separated them!"

"Yes, you did. And now it's Clara's turn."

I stared at the nine fleas left on the tea towel. This was ridiculous. If I hadn't just seen Kahla do it, I would have said it was impossible. There was no way I could do that.

"Please would you sing that song again?" I said, to gain time. "I didn't quite catch how..."

"It's not the song," Isa said. "That just makes it easier to concentrate. You don't have to sing if you don't want to."

"But then how...?"

Kahla rolled her eyes. "Which school did you go to?" she snorted.

"Kahla, be quiet," Aunt Isa said. "This is all new to Clara. And it's not her fault. Clara, start by closing your eyes."

OK, I could manage that. I did as I was told.

"Can you hear how the sounds grow louder?"

I listened. And yes, it really was as if the rustling of the trees grew a little louder. And I could hear a twig snap under Kahla's feet when she started shifting to keep warm. Was that a small snuffle coming from the basket where the hedgehog lay?

"When I tell you, cover your ears so you can't hear anything either."

"And what happens then?"

"Then you might experience something. Go on. Try."

I stuck my fingers in my ears. The rustling from the treetops disappeared. At first I heard only the sounds of my own body, but... suddenly I could smell the forest floor very strongly, a dark-brown, wet scent of rain and autumn and hedgehog. Yes. I could actually smell the hedgehog!

I opened my eyes again.

"Wow," I said. "This is what it must be like to be a dog."

"Only their sense of smell is a thousand times stronger," Isa said. "Now we'll try something else. You close your eyes. I cover your ears. And you pinch your nose."

"What happens then?"

"We'll find out. Just do it."

So there I was, now unable to see, hear or smell.

72

I could feel the cold against my skin and the soil under my boots. I could taste my own saliva. And that was all.

"Nothing's happening," I said.

"Don't stop," Aunt Isa said, holding her warm hands over my ears to cancel out all noise. *Don't stop.*

I jumped. I had heard her even though I couldn't hear her. And all at once I could hear a million sounds and a million lives – tweeting, croaking, swooping, growing, falling, flying, roaring, barking, bubbling lives. My head started spinning and I couldn't hold my balance.

"Shut up!" I screamed. "Go away."

GOAWAYGOAWAYGOAWAY! I shouted it both out loud and inside my head. Around me everything was swaying and spinning. I fell, hitting the ground with a soft, wet bump, and rolled down the hill, around and around while I got rotting leaves in my mouth and mud in-between my teeth.

Then there was silence. I was lying on my stomach up against a birch tree and all I could hear was the wind and my own gasping. Then the forest exploded.

Bumble came hurtling down the hill as fast as he could. And behind him followed an avalanche of mice, toads, beetles, squirrels, midges, dung beetles, millipedes, moths... countless birds took flight, great tits and rooks and jays and sparrows, and they were all running for their lives. The basket next to Kahla rocked frantically from side to side as the hedgehog struggled to get out so it, too, could flee.

Aunt Isa quickly got up and started singing. No soft humming this time, but a loud and clear, warm tone that stopped the panicky stampede in its tracks. Wings and legs and animal hearts calmed down. The rooks circled above our heads to tell us off, and the basket with the hedgehog stopped rocking.

I sat on the wet soil, breathing in through my mouth.

Me.

I had made this happen.

They were running away from me. Because I had told them to.

It was impossible. And yet it had happened. It wasn't something I'd made myself believe, it wasn't a random coincidence. It was *real*.

Isa took my hand and helped me back to my feet.

"Was that... was that what you wanted me to do?" I asked.

"Well..." Aunt Isa said, as she glanced around the now almost deserted hill. "At least the fleas have gone..."

CHAPTER 9

Wildways

"Where are you?" Oscar asked.

There was static crackling and hissing in my ear and he sounded very far away. But then again, so he was.

"At my aunt's." I let out a sigh.

I was sitting at the top of the hill, on the stone wall which served as the northern border of Aunt Isa's wildward. It was practically the only spot with mobile signal. Strictly speaking I should have asked for her permission before trundling up here, but I didn't want her overhearing what I had to say to Oscar. Besides, I was *almost* within the boundaries of the wildward. Nothing could go wrong, could it?

"So are you on holiday?"

"Nah. Or, yes. I guess so." It was the most bizarre holiday I'd ever had. "Are you back from the hospital now?"

"They let me go home the day before yesterday. My head still hurts, especially when I try to play *AutoCrash*, but the doctor says that will stop soon."

"That's good."

I desperately wanted to tell him how much I missed him, but I didn't. You don't say *I miss you* to a boy who isn't your boyfriend. Do you?

I could hear noises in the background. The buzz of an intercom, voices, footsteps from the stairwell. Oscar's dog, Woofer, was barking in that excited and agitated labrador-way that meant they had visitors. I heard Oscar's mum speak to someone.

"Magnus and Kit are here," Oscar said. "We're going to make popcorn and watch DVDs. I'll call you later, OK?"

I could hear he was about to hang up.

"No, wait," I called out. "You can't. I'll have to call you."

"Why?"

"Because there's no signal here. Not unless I walk up the hill where I'm sitting now."

"So where does your aunt live? Farflungistan?"

"You're only half wrong."

"All right, I'll text you instead. See you later."

And he was gone. I was left quite unreasonably envious of Kit and Magnus, who were about to veg out on the sofa cushions on the floor with Oscar and stuff themselves with popcorn and watch trash TV.

"Farflungistan," I muttered darkly to myself. "That's exactly what it is."

I trudged back down the hill. Kahla had gone home for the day. Her dad had picked her up just as he had done the other three days I'd been here. Every morning he would drop her off at the gate and every afternoon he would pick her up again. Not in a car, but on foot, so I guessed they had to live nearby.

Aunt Isa had lit a lamp and was drawing at the large table by the window, I could see. A fat mallard waddling around the table appeared to be today's model. Duck cards sold well, Aunt Isa had told me. By the looks of it, even a wildwitch needed to earn hard cash every now and then.

I didn't go inside. Aunt Isa thought I'd gone out to tend to Star, so I decided I'd better do that. Of all the animals that lived with Aunt Isa, Star was my favourite – except for Bumble. She was a small, tough, round-backed mare; not exactly a glamorous thoroughbred, but good-natured and strong, and with four sturdy legs and a bristly, upright mane that suggested there was a bit of Norwegian Fjord Horse in her somewhere.

She was grazing in the field that was sheltered by the tall trees near the brook but when I called her, she raised her head, greeted me with a happy neigh and trotted towards the gate. Her stomach and chest were plastered with mud and her golden-brown winter coat was matted from the rain.

"Come on, horsey. Let me rub you down," I said, and she followed me willingly into the stable. I tied her to one of the rings in the wall while I rubbed her fairly dry and brushed the worst of the mud off her. One of the goats came over to say hello, and Star lowered her neck and snorted at it. Because there were no other horses here, Star had adopted the goats as her herd, Aunt Isa said. They kept each other company and got on well even though they were very different. That was more than could be said for Kahla and me. I don't know why she was so snappy and angry with me all the time. If only she'd been a little nicer, living here in Farflungistan would have been much more fun and not nearly as lonely.

Grooming the horse cheered me up. Until a year ago I'd been having lessons in an old riding school by the town hall park, but then the council decided to shut it down for safety reasons, and that was the end of my having horses within a fifteen-minute bike ride. The riding school moved out of town, which meant I had to catch two different buses and it would have taken me more than an hour to get there, so now I only went when Mum had time to drive me. I missed it so much, both the horses and my riding friends, especially Mia, Laura and Anna. And Magic, who was the horse I'd ridden the most, and on whom I'd even been allowed to take part in club events. Star might not be anybody's idea of an eventer, and would probably roll around laughing if you asked her for an extended trot or tried to get her to jump over anything taller than a tree trunk, but she had a warm, soft muzzle and friendly eyes, and at least she smelled of horse. Of wet and muddy horse and a little bit of goat. She was definitely better than nothing.

While I was trying to brush the mud out of Star's thick black tail, I got a strange feeling of being watched. I looked up. Hoot-Hoot was sitting on one of the beams above me, but he wasn't the one spying on me. He flapped his wings anxiously and turned his head in that 360° way that only owls can do. Then, without warning, he took off and swooped over Star's head and mine with a shrill cry.

My heart skipped a beat. Star snorted and shook her head. One of the goats bleated nervously.

"Clara!" Aunt Isa was calling me in a sharp and very firm voice. "Get inside, now!"

I hadn't finished with Star. She still had mud in her tail and I hadn't yet given her fresh hay. But there was something in Aunt Isa's tone that made me put the brush down on the feed bin and leave the stable immediately.

It was almost as dark in the yard as it had been inside the stable. The rain was only a misty drizzle now, but the wind was rising and the branches of the chestnut tree at the end of the farmhouse were swaying and rocking. Aunt Isa was standing in the doorway with a lamp behind her and Hoot-Hoot on her shoulder, looking just as hunched as the very first time I'd seen her.

"Hurry up!" she shouted.

I ran across the yard and ducked under the door with Bumble on my heels.

"What is it?" I asked.

"The wildways have opened. I think someone's looking for you."

"The wildways?"

"I'm going out. Close the door after me and bolt it. Then go and wait in the kitchen; I'll tap on the window when I want to get back in. I won't be long."

She took a hurricane lamp, lit it and went outside. I bolted the door just like she'd told me to.

What did she mean by "the wildways have opened"? And what was she doing outside? The duck had jumped down from the table and was cowering behind the log basket. Every now and then it let out a fearful little quack, as if hoping someone would reassure it that it wasn't alone. I knew exactly how it felt. I curled up on the sofa and pressed my nose against the window to get a better look at what was going on in the November twilight outside.

I could see the bobbing beam of light from the hurricane lamp and behind it my aunt's figure, still with Hoot-Hoot on her shoulder. She was walking towards the gate and the white stones. When she reached them, she hung the lamp on a fence post and stood still for a long time. I think she was singing. I couldn't hear her, but a sense of... tranquillity began to spread. It was as if the flame in the lamp burned more steadily, as if the wind blew less fiercely and the chestnut branches scraped less angrily against the roof. The duck stopped quacking and tucked its beak under its wing.

Aunt Isa returned shortly afterwards. I think she saw my face through the glass because she didn't tap on the window as she'd said she would, but just waited until I unbolted and opened the door.

"So what happened?" I asked.

"There was unrest on the wildways," she said. "But I strengthened the boundaries of my ward and I think they're safe now."

"What's wrong with the wildways? What does that even mean?"

"Put the kettle on so we can have a cup of tea. Then I'll explain it to you."

I had a cheese sandwich with jam and a mug of tea while my aunt turned my world upside down by telling me how everything was actually connected.

"When Chimera turned up and you were nearly run over by that lorry... what happened?" she asked.

"It was foggy," I said. "We had to get off our bikes and push them because we couldn't see where we were going. Suddenly it was as if the pavement disappeared. And then she came. Out of the fog."

Aunt Isa nodded.

"That's the wildways," she said. "The fog, or rather the pathways inside it. Anything born wild uses the wildways – to hear more than it can usually hear. To hide better or to hunt better. You used them when you scared off the fleas – and the rest of the forest while you were at it." She smiled to let me know that she was only joking. "A fully fledged wildwitch can enter the wildways in the foglands in one place and come out somewhere else. That's one of the reasons why I have ward boundaries. So that only those I've invited can enter."

"Can you... walk the wildways?"

"Yes. But I don't do it very often."

"But you could? And go... anywhere you wanted?"

"Well, it's not quite that simple. For example, it's easier to find a place you've visited before. The hardest thing about the wildways is finding your way around them."

"But if you suddenly wanted to... oh, let's say, go on holiday to Barbados? Then you could do it – even though it's a really long way away?"

"I wouldn't do it just to go on holiday."

"But you could? Without buying a plane ticket? Completely free?"

She drank a mouthful of her tea and shook her head.

"Nothing is free, Clara. It costs something other than money."

"I would love to be able to do that," I said, and thought that if Aunt Isa could nip off to Barbados just like that, perhaps I could learn to make my way to the riding school without having to catch two different buses. I mean, it was much closer than Barbados.

Then I remembered Star.

"I never gave Star her hay," I said.

"We can do it together," Aunt Isa said. "I need to check up on her and the other animals. They can sense when something happens, and it makes them jittery."

I bit my lip. Just as I'd finally discovered one good thing about being a wildwitch, Isa brought me back to earth. I would clearly not be popping off to the riding school for the foreseeable future. Not as long as Chimera was waiting out there in the fog on the wildways.

"You said that someone was looking for me. Was that Chimera?"

Aunt Isa took the hurricane lamp from the hook by the door and stuck her feet in her wellies again.

"Probably," she said. "It's either Chimera – or that big black monster cat of yours."

The cat. I automatically touched my forehead, where the claw marks were still visible although the scars were now less red. I would almost rather be found by Chimera.

CHAPTER 10

Fire and Ashes

"No, Clara. Try again. Watch Kahla."

I got utterly fed up of hearing those words in the week that followed. Kahla could make fleas line up in ranks and salute her. Kahla could summon a single rook from a tree without the other birds taking off. Kahla could locate a specific ant in an anthill. And she could blend into the landscape so well that Bumble and I would walk straight past her without ever knowing she was there.

Kahla was so clever. Kahla could do everything that I couldn't do.

If only she had been nice – or even halfway friendly. But she kept scowling at me as if she would love nothing more than to turn me into a beetle and squash me.

"Are you sure you're not wrong?" I asked Aunt Isa while we gave Bumble, Star, the goats and all the other more or less resident animals their breakfast feed.

"About what?"

"About me being a wildwitch."

Yesterday Aunt Isa had told me to call Bumble wildwitch style: without saying anything and without his being able to see me. Bumble hadn't stirred from the spot. He'd just sat there by the pond on his big brown bottom, mesmerized by the acorns that plopped into the water at regular intervals. He hadn't even wagged his tail. And this was Bumble we were talking about. The world's friendliest dog. Meanwhile, Kahla was making the rooks come and go as if they were bike messengers she could simply call on her wildwitch telephone. "Rook number four from the left, yes, you with the long beak... come to me, would you?" It was driving me crazy. "It's so easy for Kahla!"

"Kahla's parents have been playing wildwitch games with her since she was three years old. You won't reach her level in a week, sweetheart."

Star buried her muzzle in the hay and started munching. I stroked her woolly neck.

"But when will I? When can I go home?"

I missed my mum and I missed Oscar. And he hadn't texted me, either, even though he'd promised. Or perhaps I hadn't got his text – who knew if things like that even worked out here in Farflungistan?

Isa looked at me. "Is this making you very upset?" she asked. "Do you hate all of it or do you enjoy some parts?"

I needed a moment to think about that because up until now I had been focusing mostly on things I found stupid, dangerous and irritating.

"I like all the animals," I said slowly. "And I like Star and Bumble. And you."

"And I like you too, Clara sweetheart."

"If it was just a holiday," I said. "If I knew that I would be going home to Mum's in a week or two, or... I mean, if I could just be sure. And if it wasn't for the cat and Chimera..." It might have been exciting to learn all this wildwitch magic if the situation hadn't been so desperate. Or if I had been any good at it. Or if Kahla had been nicer.

"Try to focus on the positive," Aunt Isa said. "And you'll have a better day."

I tried. I really did. But the day didn't care. It got off to a bad start – before it decided to go completely wrong altogether. As wrong as it could possibly go...

It was bitterly cold and raining. I was deeply envious of Kahla's seven or eight layers of clothes because, although I'd borrowed Aunt Isa's bright yellow rain hat and was wearing a nice thick sweater under my raincoat, big fat raindrops trickled steadily down my neck and under my collar, and my toes were starting to feel like two packets of mince that had just been taken out of the freezer.

We'd been given a pad and pencil in a plastic bag that stopped the paper dissolving in the rain. Our task was to sit by the willow pond, listen, sense and note down all the wildlife we could detect within a radius of fifty metres. Kahla was writing non-stop. On my pad I had written "two ducks", "blackbird" and "Bumble", and then I cheated and wrote "worms" even though that was just a guess. After that I sat gnawing my pencil while I shivered. The wind rattled the branches of the willow tree and raindrops formed circles on the surface of the dark pond. I spotted an empty snail shell between the reeds. I was fairly sure that the snail that had once lived inside it was long dead and gone, but I wrote "snail" all the same.

Then I was stuck. Opening or closing my eyes made no difference. I knew they were there – beetles under the tree bark, fish and frogs and other aquatic animals in the pond, moles and mice and small birds. But I couldn't sense them.

"How are you doing?" Aunt Isa asked us.

"Great!" Kahla exclaimed, scribbling away like mad.

"Great..." I mumbled and wrote "beetle" just to give myself something to do. How many types of beetle had Aunt Isa told us were in this part of the country? Chances were that one of them, at least, must be nearby. Were there tadpoles at this time of year? Probably not.

I snuck a peek at Kahla. She underlined something, got up and handed her notepad to Aunt Isa.

"There are plenty more further out, obviously," she said. "But you did say fifty metres only."

Aunt Isa took Kahla's notepad and started reading.

"Good work, Kahla," she said, pointing to one of the words on the list. "That one is so deep down I wasn't sure you'd be able to sense it."

I wrote "mole" on my own pad. Then I heard a contemptuous little snort behind me.

Kahla was looking over my shoulder. She could see just how few words were on my paper. And she'd caught me cheating about the mole.

She didn't say anything, but she smiled. And not in a nice, friendly way.

I lost my temper. She was laughing at me. She was standing there mocking me and it was clearer than ever that she thought I was embarrassing and hopeless and a joke. I was fed up with listening to her – and even more upset that she was right.

Get lost, I thought. Leave me alone! Shoo. *Go away.*

The ducks flapped their wings and took off in fright. And Kahla stepped back in surprise. Her foot slipped on the muddy shore and she reached out for a branch in an attempt to steady herself.

Snap! The branch broke with a wet, rotten sound and that was it. Kahla tumbled sideways into the water and briefly disappeared among the reeds and aquatic plants. Then she surfaced, spluttering and gasping, still up to the middle of her thighs in water.

"Kahla!" Aunt Isa threw down the notepad and pulled her back on land with a firm grip.

Kahla was completely drenched. All her woolly layers were soaked through and her dark hair stuck to her face in flattened black wisps. One of her rainbow-coloured Inca hats floated on the surface of the pond like a merry little boat. She stared at me with big, shocked eyes.

"You..." she said. "It was you..."

"We'll talk about it later," Aunt Isa said in a rather ominous tone of voice. "Right now we need to get you into some dry clothes."

Kahla couldn't stop shaking. Aunt Isa had filled up the old tub with steaming hot water twice now and poured mug after mug of boiling hot tea into her, but it made no difference. In the end we dressed her in practically all the clothes I'd brought with me and wasn't wearing, plus a big old woolly sweater, three pairs of socks and a pair of Aunt Isa's boots.

Kahla looked completely different without her chrysalis of multi-coloured clothes. Small, skinny and frightened, and no longer snooty. She stuck like a limpet to the stove in the living room, her lips blue from the cold. Tears rolled quietly down her cheeks.

"I want to go home," she said. "Please, let me go home."

I just stood there, fidgeting and guilty. I had a strange feeling that it was my fault, that I must have pushed Kahla somehow even though I hadn't touched her, and that was why she'd fallen into the pond. I could remember only too well what

I'd felt the moment she reappeared in the water and I realized that she wasn't drowning or seriously injured.

Triumphant.

I'd relished the moment. So much so that I had to chew the inside of my cheek to stop myself from laughing out loud.

But as I looked at her now, the joke was over.

"Are you OK?" I whispered when Aunt Isa went to the kitchen to fetch more tea.

She looked at me. She had blue and purple rims under her eyes and she was so pale that her dark skin looked almost grey.

"I c-can't handle cold," she said miserably. "It m-makes me ill."

She didn't accuse me again of making her fall in. She didn't even mention it. And she was no longer scowling at me, but that only made me feel worse.

"I'm sorry," I said. "I... I hope you don't get ill."

Aunt Isa returned with more tea.

"Drink this," she said, and thrust a full mug into Kahla's hand where the empty one had been.

"I can't drink any more," Kahla protested. "My tummy's squelching." But she took the mug all the same and folded both hands around it to warm them up. "I just want to go home, please!"

Aunt Isa studied her with a furrowed brow.

"Yes," she said eventually. "That's probably the best thing for it." Then she turned to me.

"Clara, listen to me. I have to walk Kahla home. It means I need to leave you on your own for an hour or two. I'll be as quick as I can, but it's some distance, even using the wildways."

I nodded. "That's OK."

"It'll have to be," Aunt Isa said. "Lock the door after me. Do *not* go outside. And don't let anyone in. Do you understand?"

"Yes," I said. "I'll be careful."

I meant it when I said it. But things don't always go as planned.

T ime passed. I tried reading a book, but after a while I realized that I was just turning the pages without following the story. Why wasn't Aunt Isa back yet? Surely an hour must have passed by now?

My panic increased as it grew steadily darker outside.

"Everything will be all right," I said to myself. So loud that Bumble cocked his head and looked at me as if trying to work out what those strange human noises meant. I was glad that he was here.

Had I been able to, I would have brought Star into the living room as well.

Suddenly Bumble jumped up from his place on the sofa and planted both front paws on the windowsill. He raised his hackles and let out a low, dangerous growl.

"What is it, Bumble?"

Had I ever heard him growl before? I didn't think so. It was a deep, ominous sound that made him seem like a completely different animal from the tail-wagging cuddly teddy bear that I knew.

Then Star neighed. No. She wasn't neighing – she was screaming. Shrill and frightened. And when I pushed Bumble aside and looked towards the stable, I saw long, yellow flames lick the stable door.

Petrified, I stared at them for a few seconds. What could I do? My mobile didn't work and anyway the nearest fire station was an hour away, at least. Star couldn't wait that long.

Bumble started barking. I raced to the back of the house, jumped into my boots, unlocked the door and ran into the yard.

I could see now that someone had built a small fire against the stable door. I kicked the burning branches and scattered them, and most of the flames went out. The fire hadn't properly got hold of the door itself, the scorched planks were only smouldering, but I pulled and yanked at the door until I lifted it out of its hinges, then dragged it to the middle of the yard, where the embers wouldn't reach the thatched roof if they flared up again. Star was still whinnying heartbreakingly inside the stable and one of the goats clattered out through the doorway and started running down the gravel road.

I let it run. Bumble was standing next to me, bristling and staring fixedly at the stable. His growling made his body vibrate so much that I could feel it against my leg.

Somebody did that, I thought. Somebody built a fire against the door and set it alight. On purpose.

Why? Why would anyone want to burn down the stable?

To make me leave the house.

The answer popped into my brain the very same second I spotted her.

Chimera.

She was sitting on the roof of the stable, crouching like a bird on a perch. Her wings lay folded flat against her back. Her yellow eyes glared at me. Had she been sitting there the whole time or had she only just appeared?

She's a wildwitch, I thought. She'd been there the whole time, only I hadn't been able to see her.

She spread her wings. It was as if they blacked out the whole sky. Then she launched herself from the roof and swooped down towards me. I turned around to flee, but didn't manage even two steps towards the house before she caught me.

CHAPTER 11

Blood and Red Rainbows

I've never tried being a baby rabbit caught by a bird of prey, but I think I now know how it feels. The weight of Chimera knocked me over, I fell flat on my face and couldn't breathe. Her wings shut out any light, blinding me, and her talons cut into my body like knives. Bumble's furious snarling turned into a howl of pain and then he, too, was silenced.

I don't believe I was even capable of thought. I can't remember that I had anything in my head but terror and the taste of blood.

I couldn't resist her. I couldn't raise my arms or my legs, I couldn't even try to wriggle free of her clutches. She pulled my arms behind my back and tied them with something that cut into my wrists. Then she yanked my head back and put something just as cold and sharp around my neck.

It burned against my skin and made it harder to breathe.

"Cold iron," she hissed close to my ear. "So don't even try."

I had no idea what she was talking about. Try what? And why iron? It felt more like wire.

"Get up."

I wasn't sure that I could. I was still trying to suck in air in pathetic little mouthfuls and one of my legs felt strangely anaesthetized.

Chimera didn't care. She yanked my neck, which made everything go black, and, if I wanted to carry on breathing, I would have to stand up. I succeeded on my second attempt, but when I put my weight on the numb leg, I felt a burning and pricking sensation.

The first thing I saw was Bumble.

He lay very still, reduced to a pile of fur and bones that seemed too small to be big, bear-like Bumble.

"Bumble!" I tried to reach him, but another yank stopped me. One end of the chain was attached to the iron collar around my neck and Chimera was holding the other in her hand as if it were a leash and I were a dog. "What have you done to him?"

She didn't bother replying. She just tugged the leash again so I stumbled and nearly fell over.

"Get a move on, witch child," she said. "We haven't got all day."

So I was forced to hobble after her whether I wanted to or not. Across the yard, down the gravel road, through the gate with the white stones. Without knowing what had happened to Bumble, without knowing whether he was dead or alive.

Fog enveloped us the moment we passed the white stones. It was a strange fog, not at all damp and clammy like ordinary mist, but dry like smoke – and just as dense.

Witch's fog. The fog of the wildways. I knew that now.

Chimera was in a rush. All her movements were urgent and she pulled and yanked me whenever she thought I wasn't moving fast enough, which was pretty much most of the time.

Even so, my brain was slowly starting to function again. I didn't know where we were going, but it didn't take a genius to work out that the further away we got, the smaller were the chances of Aunt Isa being able to find me again. I reckoned that explained why Chimera was in such a hurry. She was scared of Aunt Isa. And that made me a little braver in the midst of all the misery.

But what could I do? My hands were tied behind my back, I had an iron collar around my neck and she was bigger and stronger and ten times more... ten times *witchier* than me. I slowed down deliberately even though it meant more hard tugs to my poor neck, but it didn't make much difference to our progress. We continued to move further and further away from Aunt Isa's, and this wasn't a place where I could snap branches or throw breadcrumbs to leave a trail. There was nothing here but fog.

Self-defence for wildwitches, lesson one. Had I learned anything at all while I'd been with Aunt Isa?

One thing. There was only one thing I was good at. That is, if I could pull it off.

I closed my eyes. I listened with that strange inner sense that Aunt Isa had assured me I had. This place wasn't teeming with life as the forest had been. There were no beetles or worms or birds or ants. There were only the wildways and Chimera and me. I could sense her very clearly; a mixture of hot and cold, a strange, red rainbow, and I could smell wet feathers and blood.

"Go away," I whispered.

She actually stopped for a moment. She came closer to me.

"What?" she said. "What are you doing, you witch brat?"

Then I screamed. I summoned up all the strength I had inside me and screamed at the top of my voice, the same scream that had caused the whole forest to stampede.

GO AWAY.

She started screaming, too. A shrill cry of anger, thin and piercing like a bird of prey's. She flapped her wings and a hard edge of feathers hit my face and blinded me for a brief moment. But I didn't need to be able to see in order to shout.

GOAWAYGOAWAYGOAWAY...

"Blood of Viridian!" she hissed. No, more than hissed – she spat the words like a curse. She backed away, one step at a time. It seemed that she couldn't bear to be near me. She yanked the chain one last time, so forcefully that it felt as if my head were going to be ripped off, but when that failed to make me stop, she dropped the chain as if it were red hot.

"I'll get you next time..."

Only her words lingered in the air. Chimera herself was no longer there.

I kept shouting *GOAWAY* long after I knew that she'd gone. Long after I could sense that I was on my own. Alone in the fog of the wildways. I didn't stop until I was absolutely sure I couldn't smell blood or sense the slightest trace of red rainbows.

My neck and my throat hurt. My hands felt cold and dead. One of my knees was almost refusing to carry me. But that wasn't the worst.

The most difficult thing about the wildways is navigating them.

That was what Aunt Isa had said. And I believed her. The fog that had swallowed up Chimera now closed around me like a sack. I didn't know what direction I should start walking in. There *were* no directions.

How on earth would I find my way home?

CHAPTER 12

Purring Cats

"Think, Clara, think."

I spoke the words slowly and out loud because it was important. There was absolutely no point in walking without knowing where I was going. My knee hurt like crazy and I didn't know how many steps I could take on it before it would refuse to carry me any further.

At home – I mean, back home in the normal world where I'd lived until a couple of weeks ago – Mum and I had agreed that if anything happened that I couldn't handle, all I had to do was call her and she would come and get me. But I had no mobile here and no way of contacting Mum.

What was here apart from fog?

There was silence. All I could hear was a faint whooshing sound that could easily have been the blood in my ears. There were no smells now except my own smell of sweat and fear. It was neither hot nor cold, dry nor damp. There was nothing.

It reminded me of something.

I remembered how Aunt Isa had made me close my eyes and pinch my nose while she covered my ears. How she had taken away all my senses, one by one, until only my wildsense remained.

It was all I had now.

I probably didn't need to close my eyes, but I did it anyway. I stood very still in the wildfog and tried to listen. Something must live in this wasteland – apart from Chimera, that was.

I strained as hard as I could to hear, I extended my wildsense into the fog, exploring and searching. If I'd had any other option, I probably wouldn't even have tried. But there was no plan B, so I carried on even though I was so tired I was swaying with exhaustion and hot tears were streaming down my face. I kept trying. And at last...

Here.

Very, very faintly. A little warmth, a little distant voice. *Here I am.*

Was that Aunt Isa looking for me? I didn't recognize the sound or whatever you would call it, but at least it wasn't Chimera and, as long as it wasn't her, it could be anyone else, for all I cared.

I started walking while continuing to listen out for the faint calling. My knee hurt and there was still no trail or path to follow, only fog. But my sense of the calling voice grew stronger and stronger.

It was soon after that my knee refused to carry on. It buckled under me and I collapsed, unable, because of the chain, to brace my fall with my hands. The fall itself didn't really hurt because there was neither grass nor stone nor soil under my feet; all I landed on was a kind of firmer fog. But I couldn't get back up again.

Find me, I prayed in silence. Please find me. I can't go on.

Out of the fog a creature appeared. I could see that it wasn't human, but it wasn't until it got very close that I recognized it.

It was the cat.

I wanted to shout **GOAWAY** at it, too, but I couldn't. I was spent. I just lay there with my hands chained behind my back and a knee that refused to obey me. The cat could do whatever it wanted, I was helpless.

It was just as big as I remembered. As big as a dog or a small panther. Black as night and bushy with wet pearls of dew in its fur. It no longer smelled strongly of seaweed, there was just a faint hint of salt water. But its eyes were still as yellow. It opened its mouth in a pink yawn that revealed glistening teeth and stretched out lazily. It strolled towards me, languid and relaxed, as if it knew that I couldn't do anything, couldn't fight back, couldn't escape.

Mine, it said, sounding contented, just like in my nightmares. *Mine.*

Then it lay down next to me, very close.

And began to purr.

At first I didn't understand what it was doing. For several minutes I expected it to sink its claws into me or bite my neck.

It didn't. It lay purring against my stomach, and its body heat spread to me as if someone had lit a campfire. And slowly I realized that it didn't want to hurt me. At least, not now. I had no idea why it was suddenly helping me rather than hunting me, nor was I sure I could trust that things would stay that way. But right here and right now it looked after me as if I were a kitten and it my mum.

"Who are you?" I whispered.

But it made no reply. It merely purred a little louder.

And this was how Aunt Isa found us at last.

CHAPTER 13

The Coven Gathers

Aunt Isa's living room seemed smaller than usual. That was because it was full of wildwitches. Aunt Isa had told me who they were and introduced us, but the names floated around my head and refused to settle and attach themselves to anyone in particular. The elderly gentleman with the beard and tweed jacket was Mr Malkin, I believed, and I was fairly certain that the nice lady with the round, ruddy cheeks and the chalk-white hair was Mrs Pommerans. But what on earth was the name of the young woman with the green-and-black-striped hair? The one who looked like a Goth with black eye make-up and safety pins in her ears, and trousers with so many holes that her knees stuck out through the fabric. An all-white ferret had draped itself around her neck and was watching the rest of us with blood-red eyes.

Then there was Kahla and her dad, whom everybody called Master Millaconda. He seemed to be just as sensitive to the cold as Kahla because he hadn't taken off his long brown camel-hair coat even though the fire was roaring in the stove and the windows had steamed up with condensation from the heat of the visitors.

They had been out looking for me. It was a humbling thought and I knew I ought to be grateful, but right now I just wanted them all to go home so the house could return to normal and I could be alone with Aunt Isa and Bumble, who was lying on a quilt in front of the stove, still weak and confused after Chimera's attack. But alive, luckily.

I was so tired. Aunt Isa had sung wildsongs for me and stroked my neck, my knee and my wrists, but everything was still aching and swollen. My mind, too, felt achy and swollen, as if I'd sprained something in my head when I shouted **GOAWAY** at Chimera. I could do with another helping of my aunt's magic. And I had so many questions.

One of them was about the big, black creature stretched out on the sofa, lying along my leg and resting its wide head on my lap. *Mine* it purred at regular intervals even though it was quite obviously more than half asleep. *Mine, mine, mine.* The tip of its tail flipped from side to side in lazy, contented jerks. I didn't know what to make of it. Aunt Isa said that the cat had most likely saved my life by staying with me and emitting its big, black, furry distress signal. And yet it was the same cat that had scratched me and licked my blood and given me Cat Scratch Disease. What was going on? I really wanted to ask Aunt Isa about that.

The strange wildwitches, however, showed no signs of leaving. Quite the contrary. They had only just begun their meeting. And the main topic on the agenda – well, it was me. Me and Chimera.

"Perhaps you would be kind enough to tell us what happened, Miss Clara," said Beardy, whose real name might be Mr Malkin. And, of course, everyone turned to look at me – both people and animals. I went bright red with embarrassment, and hunched over my teacup to hide it.

"I locked the door just like Aunt Isa told me to," I said without looking at them. "But then I saw something burning outside the stable…"

I told them about the fire that had been built right up against the stable door and about Star screaming from inside. Even now when I knew that it was a ploy by Chimera to get me out of the house, I still couldn't see how I could have done anything other than what I did. After all, I couldn't let her burn down the stable with Star and all the goats inside... just the thought of it made the tears well up in my eyes.

"Of course not," said Mrs Pommerans, who was sitting next to me on the sofa. "You're a good girl and a brave one, Clara, and you did what you had to do." She comforted me by stroking my arm, which did indeed seem to help, while a scented cloud of peppermint spread around her. She had called me brave. No one had ever done that before. The lump in my throat grew smaller and after a few deep breaths I could carry on without crying.

"She was perching on the roof," I said. "I didn't see her to begin with, but then suddenly there she was. And then... then she flew right at me."

Mr Malkin raised an eyebrow.

"I thought her wings were mostly decorative," he said. "Can she actually fly?"

Master Millaconda shook his head.

"She shouldn't be able to. If they really were able to support her weight, the wingspan would have to be four to five times greater. But they probably give her the ability to glide."

I looked hesitantly from one to the other.

"She flew," I said. "From the roof and down... down on top of me. I... I fell. And she tied my hands and put a collar around my neck so that

111

I couldn't resist very much, and she... she did something to Bumble."

Aunt Isa nodded.

"She bewitched him," she said. "She twisted his life cord. He was still unconscious when I came home. Without my help, I don't think he would have made it." Bumble's tail bashed the floor softly. Either he knew that we were talking about him or he was just pleased to hear Aunt Isa's voice.

"What does that mean?" I asked. "His... life cord?"

"All living beings have something inside them which we call the life cord," Mrs Pommerans explained. "It's where your life force comes from and it's what connects us to the rest of the living world. If it breaks, we die."

So Bumble had nearly died. She had almost killed him. It made me so angry that the teacup clattered in my hand.

"She's mean," I said. "She's mean and evil and... she doesn't care about anyone."

The Goth girl nodded. "She's as cold as ice. She doesn't give a damn about the rest of the world as long as she gets what she wants."

"Shanaia speaks from experience," Mrs Pommerans said. "She lost her home because of Chimera."

Shanaia. That was her name. She was sitting astride one of the dining chairs, resting her arms on its back. Her eyes shone white in the middle of all the black make-up and she wore black, fingerless leather gloves with studs along the knuckles. I felt quite intimidated by Shanaia and her ferret and was relieved that she was with us against Chimera and not vice-versa. I was just about to ask her how she had lost her home, but Mr Malkin went on with his questions.

"Miss Clara, please continue. We have important decisions we need to make tonight."

So I had to tell them the rest. How Chimera dragged me off onto the wildways and how I finally made her go away.

"Interesting," Mr Malkin murmured as he stroked his beard with one hand. "Isa, dear, please may I see the iron collar? You brought it back, I trust?"

"Yes," Aunt Isa said, handing him a canvas bag into which she had put the collar and the wire once she'd freed me from them.

He opened the bag and peered into it. Then he carefully shook the contents out onto the coffee table. He took a pen from the chest pocket of his tweed jacket and poked at the thin metal chain, making sure not to touch it with his fingers.

"Cold iron," he said. "No doubt about it. And even so it didn't work. How strange."

What did he mean "it didn't work"? My throat still hurt, as did my neck, and if Aunt Isa hadn't found me, the collar would still be locked around my neck – I would never have been able to get it off on my own.

Aunt Isa had noticed my confusion.

"Cold iron cancels out magic," she said. "Most wildwitches would struggle to use their powers if they'd been chained with that thing there. But you could."

That seemed very strange given what a useless wildwitch I was.

"The only thing I'm good at is shouting *go away*," I protested.

"Yes. For now, at least. However, that is something you do with great skill."

Mr Malkin pushed the iron back in the bag, still without touching it directly.

"This is our proof," he said. "The Raven Mothers won't be able to ignore this."

"The Raven Mothers?" I said. "Who are they?"

"The wildworld's supreme council and court," Mr Malkin said. "Up until now they've hesitated, but this time they'll have to do something about Chimera!"

114

"But that means Clara would have to bear witness," Mrs Pommerans said. "Isa, do you think she's ready for that?"

My aunt looked at me with that searchlight stare from which there was no hiding.

"She's not a little mouse anymore," she said, at last. "Are you, Clara?"

The cat on my lap yawned and stretched out a paw towards my face – not to hurt me, but to demand that I scratch its stomach. I did what it asked.

"I don't think so," I said. But I wasn't entirely sure.

CHAPTER 14

Raven Kettle

"M_{um?}"

"Hello, Mouse! How are you?"

"Fine."

Why did I say that? She was thrilled to hear from me, but she was so far away. If I told her how I really felt, it would just make her sad. That was probably why I said I was fine.

"Are you having a nice time with Aunt Isa?"

"Yes. Yes, it's nice here. I really like the animals. But I... I can't wait to come home."

"I know, darling. What does Aunt Isa say? Is it safe yet?"

"I might be able to come home in a few days. If... if everything goes to plan. And... if you'll let me bring back a cat."

"A cat?"

"Er, yes. It's a long story. Please?"

There was silence at the other end. I heard a teaspoon chatter against a coffee cup.

"OK," Mum said slowly. "I suppose that would be all right. As long as you promise you'll look after it yourself."

"Yes, I promise."

"Is Aunt Isa there?"

"She's busy chatting to some guests," I said quickly. "I'll see you soon. Love you."

I hung up while she was still saying goodbye. I really wanted to call Oscar too, but it was time to go.

A motley crew had gathered at the gate by the white stones. I was riding Star to avoid putting pressure on my bad knee. Everyone else was on foot except Mrs Pommerans, who rode an old-fashioned, racing-green bicycle whose basket was decorated with flowers.

"My hip plays up if I walk too much," she said apologetically when she caught me looking at her. "I'm better on a bike."

Kahla's dad took hold of Star's reins.

"I do know how to ride, actually," I said, a little offended.

"That's good to know," he said. "But riding on

the wildways isn't quite the same as a gentle trot through the woods."

"We need to stick together," Mr Malkin added. "But if we do get separated, Master Millaconda knows where we're going. You don't."

I remembered what it had been like to wander the wildways alone without knowing which was up or down, left or right. I shuddered and suddenly I didn't mind Kahla's dad holding Star, although Kahla was standing right next to us and watching me being led by the rein like a little kid. She peered up at me from under her woolly hat, but she didn't look very arrogant now. More confused and fearful, I thought. Exactly how I felt.

"Is everyone ready?" Mr Malkin said. "Good. Let's go."

Star trudged along the gravel road with the field on one side and the spruces on the other. Then Mr Malkin and Mrs Pommerans started humming and slowly the fog across the field grew denser and greyer. Soon the fog of the wildways had enveloped us and I could see no further than Star's neck and ears, Kahla's red-and-yellow-striped woolly hat, the back of her dad's camel-hair coat and Aunt Isa right in front of us. Hoot-Hoot was perched on her shoulder, rubbing his beak against her hair. It was probably meant to be an affectionate gesture, but it looked as if he were trying to wipe something off.

The black cat rested on a fleece behind the saddle. I could feel its warm body against my back.

At regular intervals Mr Malkin, who led the way, would hum some notes. They would be repeated first by Mrs Pommerans, then by Isa and Kahla's dad, and finally by Shanaia, who was bringing up the rear. I had learned by now what all the humming and chanting was about – it was to do with finding our way and keeping our little group together in the fog of the wildways. If I closed my eyes, I could just about make out the others with my wildsense – people as well as animals. But it took a lot of energy and I felt dizzy and started to sway on Star's broad back. I decided to stop.

Suddenly something cold and wet landed on my nose. I squinted at it and saw that it was a snowflake. The fog around us was no longer just dull fog; it glistened as large, fraying, white flakes fell around us and settled on our hair and clothes and on Star's warm neck.

"Are we nearly there yet?" I asked Master Millaconda.

He nodded.

"Not long to go now," he said.

The fog dispersed. We were still in the middle of a forest, but I could see at once that it wasn't Aunt Isa's forest. This forest was ancient, with black, crooked trees whose trunks were so thick that it would have taken at least three people to reach their arms around them. And it was proper winter here, not merely late November cold. Snow covered the gnarled branches like soap suds, the path we were following was nothing but a trampled track, and the sky I could make out beyond the black treetops was gunmetal grey and laden with even more snow. Above our heads we heard the hoarse cries of birds, and wings flapping, wet from the snow, but these weren't rooks like the ones around Aunt Isa's house, these birds were much bigger.

"Oh, no," Kahla sighed to herself. "It's already winter here..."

I could tell from her voice exactly how cold she was and I felt very sorry for her in the midst of everything.

One of the big birds swooped down so close to Star's ears that I could make out every feather. Its beak was as long as my hand, its eyes shiny and jet-black. The birds circling us were ravens and I had a tingling sensation that not only were they watching us, they were also talking about us.

Behind my back the cat stretched out and then leapt lightly and elegantly down onto the ground.

"Hey, where are you going?" I asked. But it merely had another stretch before disappearing in-between the trees.

"Cats go their own ways," Master Millaconda said. "If you wind up with one of those for your wildfriend, you don't own a cat, the cat owns you."

"I'm not sure that I even chose him to begin with," I said.

"No, that's what I just said. Cats make up their own minds."

The snow was so heavy that Mrs Pommerans had to get off her bicycle and push.

"This road gets longer every time," she muttered.

"We're nearly there," Aunt Isa said. "Look – you can see the birds circling Raven Kettle now."

And we could. Just ahead of us, the sky was packed with birds. Mostly ravens, but also other, smaller silhouettes – crows, rooks and jackdaws, judging by the thousands of raucous cries that filled the air. It was like a storm of birds, a circling, black whirlwind of birds. That must be why this place was called Raven Kettle.

Or it explained the raven part. I didn't understand the kettle bit until we came closer. The path met a cart track and the cart track turned into a sunken road that reminded me of the one leading to Aunt Isa's farmhouse. The sunken road sloped down more and more deeply and the verges grew steeper and steeper until we suddenly arrived at an open space. The sides around it rose like those of a quarry and I could see we were at the bottom of a crater. In the middle there was a circle of trees, and all around the kettle walls there were windows and doors with, presumably, caves or some other kind of dwellings behind them. Light poured out through the panes and there was a smell of log fires and some sort of food.

It wasn't until we reached the centre of the circle that the noise ceased. The bird tornado stopped squawking and settled down in a swoosh of wings, as if our arrival were the signal they'd been waiting for. The birds watched us from every angle – from the circle of trees in the crater and from the branches of the trees that grew all the way around the edge at the top. It made me really quite nervous: all those eyes, all those beaks.

A door was opened and a tall woman dressed in black came out and walked to the centre of the crater.

"Good evening," she said. "Welcome. Where is the new one?"

"Here," Aunt Isa said. "This is my sister's daughter, Clara Ash. Clara, this is Thuja, who heads the Council of the Raven Mothers."

One of the ravens flew down and settled on Thuja's shoulder. It was so big that it towered over her head. It turned to examine me.

"Oh, yes. I see her now. She looks a little like you, Isa."

But Thuja wasn't looking at me. She was still facing the grey, snow-heavy sky and her eyes were closed. Suddenly I realized that she must be blind. But then how could she know that I looked like Isa?

Because she was seeing me through the eyes of the raven. It was the only explanation I could think of. I shuddered in a way that had nothing to do with the cold.

"Let's get business out of the way first," she said. "Clara Ash, you wish to accuse a witch of the wildworld. Is that right?"

I grew shy again, possibly because she was so serious.

"Yes," I whispered.

"State the name of the witch you're accusing."

"Chimera." It was a half-strangled little squeak, but at least I managed to get it out.

"Thank you," Thuja said with a certain satisfaction in her voice, as if she'd been waiting for this moment for a long time. "The Council will summon Chimera! Now come inside where it's warm while we wait, and get the fog of the wildways out of your bones."

She walked towards one of the glass doors and the others followed. I hesitated.

"What about Star?" I whispered to Aunt Isa.

"Star is welcome, too," Thuja said without turning around. "She has travelled just as far as you have."

Aunt Isa smiled up at me.

"Jump down and let's take the saddle and the reins off her," she said. "Star will decide for herself whether she wants to be inside or out."

And this was how Star ended up trotting happily after us through a glass door that opened into a large room with a fireplace in one of Raven Kettle's guest caves. The fire was already lit and ten armchairs had been arranged in a semicircle around it. A corner of the floor was covered with a thick layer of wood shavings. There was a large bucket of water and a net filled with hay, which filled the dimly lit room with the scents of meadow and summer.

"Oh, they know how to look after both their human and their animal guests here," Mrs Pommerans said, and flopped into one of the armchairs with a grateful sigh just as Star knelt on her front legs, lay down on her side and started rolling around energetically and joyfully on the wood shavings.

I limped across the room and took a seat. My knee felt stiff and it was throbbing painfully, but even so there was something about the room and the whole place that comforted me. A kettle was bubbling over the fireplace. There was no doubt that someone had prepared this peculiar mix of living room and stable for us – they must have known we were coming.

"I trust you'll find everything you need here," Thuja said. "Otherwise just let us know. We'll dispatch a messenger to Chimera. She must present herself within three days or we'll try the case without her."

"Thank you," Aunt Isa said.

"Do you think she'll come?" I asked, and couldn't help wishing that she would stay away.

"Being shunned by the wildworld is a very serious matter – even for Chimera," Aunt Isa said. "She'll come."

To my ears it sounded more like a threat than a promise.

I was so tired that I could barely eat my dinner. The beds in the guest cave were in small alcoves set into the walls and could be screened off with heavy velvet drapes. As soon as we'd eaten and I'd had a quick bath in Raven Kettle's guest bathroom, I crawled under the duvet in the alcove I shared with Kahla. She seemed to have been just as tired as I was, because she had skipped her bath and was already asleep under a pile of blankets and duvets so high that all I could see of her was a single black lock of hair. I curled up on one side and yawned a couple of times while I half-listened to the voices coming from the main room.

"... risk that they find her not guilty," Master Millaconda said.

"Impossible!" Shanaia exclaimed. "She's guilty as hell!"

"But she's not stupid," Mrs Pommerans remarked. "Remember how she got you thrown out of Westmark. They chose to believe her over you."

"But now they must realize how wrong they were!"

There was a pause. I looked up at the ceiling, which was a mesh of tree roots and moss, and felt my whole body growing heavier and heavier with each breath I took. My eyelids started closing.

"We have the neck iron," Shanaia persisted. "Surely that must count for something."

"Only if Clara gives evidence," Master Milla-conda said.

"Everything depends on the girl," Mrs Pommerans declared. "I really hope she's up to it."

So do I, I thought, and drifted off into a restless, nightmarish sleep where Chimera chased me through foggy streets and basement corridors and swooped down on me like a sparrowhawk every time I thought I'd escaped from her.

In the middle of the night I suddenly felt a furry body next to me, a warm, heavy and purring presence. My cat. My black cat.

It wasn't until then that the nightmares stopped.

CHAPTER 15

Tooth and Claw

"Clara. Clara, wake up. She's already here."

Who? What? I surfaced slowly from the depths of a black lake of sleep. Was I late for school again?

But it wasn't my mum stroking my shoulder to rouse me. It was Aunt Isa. And I wasn't in my own soft bed at home, but in one of the guest beds at Raven Kettle.

Finally I realized who she meant.

"Chimera? She's here?"

"Yes. And she's demanding that the trial begin within the hour."

My head felt fuzzy, my knee hurt.

"Does she get to decide that?"

"Yes. It's her right as we have brought charges against her."

After what Thuja had said, I'd expected to have at least three days' peace. Three days to recover, three days to prepare and find out what would happen and what it meant to bear witness before the Council of Raven Mothers. "I really hope she's up to it," Mrs Pommerans had said when she thought I was out of earshot. Everything I knew about court cases I'd learned from TV series and I had a feeling that this wouldn't be quite the same.

And it wasn't. Firstly, there was no courtroom – in fact there was no room at all. Everything took place in the middle of Raven Kettle, within the circle of snow-covered trees. Nor were there smart lawyers leaping to their feet and shouting "objection!" whenever someone badgered the witness. Where I would normally expect to see the judge, I saw seven figures all dressed in black with black headscarves – five women, of which Thuja was one, as well as two men. Most of them had a raven either on their arm or on their shoulder, and several hundred crows, ravens, rooks, and jackdaws were perched in the trees.

"Those are the Raven Mothers," whispered Aunt Isa, who was standing behind me.

"But... some of them are men...?"

"Yes, it's all equal opportunity these days."

"And some of them are blind?"

"Yes. In the old days you had to give your eyes to the ravens to become a Raven Mother. We

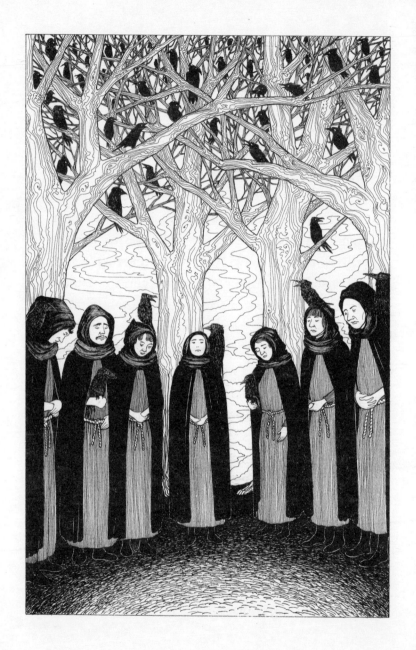

don't do that any more, fortunately, but many people born blind are drawn to this occupation, and that's understandable. I trust you've noticed how Thuja's raven is her eyes?"

I nodded.

"But... what did they do in the past? How exactly did they... *give* their eyes to the ravens?"

"Quite literally, I'm afraid. Their eyeballs would be removed and fed to the ravens. Today it's purely symbolic – just a little blood and some tears mixed with bird food which the ravens then eat."

Yuck. I didn't fancy the ravens eating any part of me, even if it was just a little blood and a few tears.

Then I remembered how the cat had licked my blood the first time we met. I couldn't see with its eyes like Thuja could with her raven's. But maybe that explained why I could hear it.

Chimera was nowhere to be seen. An hour had passed and the trial was about to start. The sun was rising and hanging low behind the trees; a great, white mist lingered at the bottom of Raven Kettle. It was so cold that I could see my own breath, but at least it had stopped snowing.

Having kept me warm all night, the cat had disappeared once more. It was as if it didn't like Raven Kettle and all the black birds. This made me uneasy, or rather even more uneasy than I already was. Downright scared, in fact. I had a hard, rough lump in my throat as if I'd swallowed a stone.

No one checked their watches or anything like that. Nevertheless I began to sense a certain impatience among the seven Raven Mothers – the she-mothers as well as the he-mothers – who were waiting among the trees. Aunt Isa was standing behind me, so close that I could feel the warmth of her body, and a little further away stood Mr Malkin, Mrs Pommerans, Master Millaconda and Shanaia. They were witnesses to some of the things Chimera had done, but I think they were there just as much to show support for me. Aunt Isa held the bag with the neck iron in her hand. Kahla wasn't there, probably because she wasn't yet a fully-fledged wildwitch, so she had stayed indoors in the guest cave with Star. Lucky so-and-so.

Then Chimera arrived.

She was enormous. Or rather her wingspan was. When she unfurled her wings, they seemed to reach from one side of the tree circle to the other.

"Let's not waste any more time," she said, as if we were late and not her. "You all know the ancient law. I demand that you surrender this little liar

to my mercy for slander and false accusations."
She pointed a long, golden claw at me.

What? *Surrendered to my mercy?*

"What does that mean?" I whispered to Aunt
Isa. "Can she do that?"

It took a while before Aunt Isa replied. "I don't
know," she said. "It's not how we usually do things
nowadays, but..."

I saw the Raven Mothers lean towards each
other in consultation. We were too far away to be
able to hear what they were whispering. Then they
straightened up and Thuja took a step forwards.

"To which law are you referring, Chimera?"

Chimera held up an old book.

"*Tooth and Claw,*" she said. "The oldest of them
all. Bravita Bloodling wrote it down four hundred
years ago, but it has existed through all times. And
it still applies."

Chimera threw the book at Thuja's feet, but
the blind Raven Mother made no attempt to pick
it up.

"First you must prove your case," she said.

I turned to Aunt Isa.

"What does she mean? Does it or does it not
apply, this *Tooth and Claw* stuff?"

"I hadn't expected this," Aunt Isa said, and
her lips were now two thin grey lines. "Nobody

drags up Bravita Bloodling in court these days, for goodness' sake."

"But what does it mean? That if we lose, then... then she'll get me?"

"In the old days being accused in front of the Council was a very serious matter. A lot of crimes carried the death penalty, so it was important that people didn't start cases out of mischief or make false accusations. The law says that the loser becomes the property of the winner, should the accusation prove to be false."

"For how long?"

"I don't know. Possibly for the rest of their life."

Suddenly my skin felt too tight all over. As if there was no longer room for both my terror and me. I didn't want to become Chimera's property. Not even for an hour. And certainly not for the rest of my life!

Aunt Isa placed a reassuring hand on my shoulder.

"That will only happen if the decision of the Council goes against us. And we have a strong case."

That was easy for her to say. She wouldn't become Chimera's slave if we lost.

I looked at Chimera. She was standing with her wings folded now – not quite as enormous as when she swept into the circle, but still gigantic. Her face was completely devoid of expression, but she stretched the fingers of one hand – or talons, rather – and clenched them again as if she was looking forward to getting her claws into me.

"Let us hear the charge," Thuja said.

I felt absolutely tiny. I don't know if it makes sense, but sometimes it feels as if everyone else is at least a head taller than me and a hundred times cleverer, braver and better looking. I'm not very tall, but my height isn't the real problem here. Sometimes it's as if I'm smaller on the inside as well. And everyone else is a giant.

I was a mouse. Or something even smaller – a beetle, an ant. I knew that if I tried to open my mouth, no sound would come out.

Aunt Isa gently nudged my back.

"You have to say it," she said. "You're the one she's offended against."

But I couldn't. My tongue was a stone in my mouth, hard, smooth, and unmoving.

Thuja raised one eyebrow and repeated her command.

"Clara Ash, let the Council hear your charge!" *Say it!*

This last voice belonged to the cat. But where was it? I looked around and spotted it just outside the circle of trees. It lay curled up, jet black against the white snow, thrashing its tail as if it wanted to lunge at Chimera's face and rip her apart with its teeth and claws.

The stone in my mouth melted. There was something about the cat's fearless spirit that seemed to rub off on me. It had my blood inside it. And maybe I had a little of the cat inside me now?

"Just tell them what happened yesterday," whispered Aunt Isa behind me.

I nodded.

"At the moment I'm living with Aunt Isa," I said.

"Louder," one of the male Raven Mothers grunted. "Tell the girl to speak up. It's impossible to hear her."

"Yesterday, while my aunt was out, Chimera came," I said, desperately trying to speak loudly and clearly.

"What? What's she saying?"

"Be quiet, Valla, and let the girl speak," Thuja said. "Surely your raven will lend you its ears if your own are no good."

The man, apparently called Valla, looked offended, but I was glad that Thuja had come to my defence.

"She set fire to the stable door to make me go outside," I said. "And then she attacked me and tied my hands with wire and put this around my neck."

Aunt Isa stepped forward and shook the neck iron out of the bag. A murmur rippled through the Raven Mothers when they realized what it was.

"A neck iron," Thuja said. "She put cold iron around your neck?"

"Yes," I said. "And she nearly killed Bumble!"

"Bumble?" Valla snarled. "Who on earth is that?"

"Our dog. She... Aunt Isa, remind me, what's it called, what she did?"

"She twisted his life cord," Aunt Isa said. "We only just managed to save his life. My home. My dog. My sister's daughter. She has offended against me too!"

Thuja shook her head.

"Isa, you can't speak for your sister-daughter. She's the accuser here, not you. You can't speak on her behalf."

Aunt Isa bowed her head and fell silent. But her hand remained on my shoulder.

"Clara, continue. What happened then?"

"Chimera tried to abduct me. She left Bumble to die and then she dragged me out on the wildways. I don't know where she would have taken me or what she would have done to me. I made her... go away. And... and in the end Aunt Isa found me."

"Still with the iron around her neck," Aunt Isa said.

"Isa..."

"I'm not making an accusation," Isa said. "I'm merely bearing witness. I saw it with my own eyes."

"Very well then. I'll allow it. So the charge is that Chimera breached Isa's wildward unlawfully, damaged her house, injured her animals and – this is the most serious charge – put another witch in cold iron."

"Yes," I said as loud as I could. "That's the charge."

Well sung, little sister, whispered the black cat in my mind. Its approval filled me with a fierce, wild heat against the chill of the winter morning.

But it was too soon to celebrate. Now it was Chimera's turn.

She unfurled her wings and slowly closed them again. Even though she didn't flap them, the snow still whirled up and danced around her feet.

"If that's all," she said, "then why are we even here?"

"Those are serious charges," Thuja said.

"If they were true. And if they were made by a witch."

"What do you mean?"

"I've come here today because I respect the Council and the law. But since when does the law say that a witch has to allow her honour to be tainted by a pathetic and confused little girl who can't even summon a mouse? She's no wildwitch. She shouldn't be standing here today and her so-called charge is a lie from start to finish. I've no idea who set fire to Isa's stable door – perhaps the girl did it herself? Nor do I know who hurt Isa's dog. Perhaps the girl is responsible for that, too. But I do know that the honoured mothers of this Council are wise enough to see through her allegation and know it for the lie that it is. Take a look at her. And then look at me. She claims she made me go away – presumably with some incantation, we're supposed to believe. And all this with cold iron around her neck. That would, in truth, require a wildwitch with extraordinary powers. Look at her, honoured Council – is that plausible?"

"No," Valla muttered. "It sounds most peculiar."

"Clara isn't lying," Isa said. "And she's a very special kind of wildwitch, she just isn't—"

"Isa, I warned you," Thuja said. "In the witches' Council it's not a question of who can afford the most expensive lawyers. Here, each witch speaks her own case."

"And those who aren't witches don't speak at all," Valla said. "Perhaps that's why the girl finds it hard to speak loudly enough for us to hear her. Can we start by clarifying whether she even is a wildwitch? Tell her to call some animal."

I stood with my mouth hanging open and a sense that the earth had just disappeared beneath my feet. Chimera had beaten me to the ground, tied me up and abducted me – and yet suddenly *I* was the accused. Of not being a wildwitch. And perhaps I wasn't. After all – who had ever heard of a wildwitch who could only shout **GOAWAY**?

"A mouse," Chimera said triumphantly. "Make her call a mouse. If she fails, she's not a witch and then it will be obvious that the rest of her story can't be true, either. And then she's mine!"

Her eyes glittered with greed and she made that gesture with her claw again.

My mind went completely blank. I didn't have one single thought, not one single emotion except undiluted panic and a desperate little voice screaming *I can't do it, I can't do it*. Far away I heard Mrs Pommerans sigh a hopeless little "Oh no..."

"My sister's daughter has only just started her training," Isa said. "She's better at making animals go away..."

"Anyone who shouts loud enough can do that," Valla said. "Now get her to call that mouse so we can proceed."

I closed my eyes and tried very hard to use my wildsense, but all I could feel was my own terror. Or so it was until I became aware of something running up my trouser leg. In amazement I opened my eyes and almost forgot to be scared. Something was darting up under my jumper and moving down the sleeve, pressing its tiny, warm claws against my skin. I held out my hand with the palm facing upwards and a thin, little grey mouse ran out of my sleeve.

I don't know where it came from. I really don't.

It just sat there on the palm of my hand and groomed its pink nose with tiny grey mouse paws. Its whiskers vibrated against my fingers. There was no way it could be the pencil case mouse, but it looked exactly like it.

"Ah, well," Valla said, sounding almost disappointed. "At least we know one thing. The girl *is* a wildwitch. Now all we have to do is find out whether she's telling the truth."

Chimera looked absolutely furious. She hadn't expected me to be able to do it. And to be honest, I don't think I did do it. It didn't feel like I had done anything. But the mouse was there and right now that was all that mattered.

"Fine," Chimera said at last. "She might be a witch. But she's still a liar. I demand trial by wildfire so that everyone can see who's telling the truth and who's lying."

"Trial by wildfire?" Thuja said. "That's a hard test for so young a witch."

"If she really is a witch and *if* she's telling the truth," Chimera said, "...then she has nothing to be scared of, does she?"

CHAPTER 16

To Run From a Fight

I guess I'd imagined I would be walking on hot coals or snuffing out a candle with my fingers or carrying something that was burning. But I was wrong.

"The trial has four parts," Mrs Pommerans explained while we sat in the guest cave waiting for darkness to fall – because a trial by wildfire has to be undertaken at night, obviously. So that you could see the flames properly, I presumed. "Skyfire, Waterfire, Earthfire and Heartfire."

Four trials – surely one was enough?

"The first part isn't too bad," Master Millaconda said, thinking he was being helpful. "It's Skyfire and they're only fireflies."

Fireflies. That didn't sound very dangerous.

"What do I do with them?" I asked, while with one hand I stroked the cat's back.

"Every trial is pretty much the same: you need to speak to some creatures and convince them that you're telling the truth. If you succeed, they'll let you pass without burning you."

"But... I don't know how to talk to them. I can only make things go away."

"Who knows – it might just work," Mrs Pommerans said with a little smile. "I've a feeling you're capable of more than you think. After all, the mouse came to you, didn't it?"

"Yes." But how could I explain that it hadn't come because I called it? It had just... appeared. Of its own accord. And possibly because I'd helped the mouse in my pencil case. What did I know? I hadn't talked to it. And I wouldn't know how to talk to the fireflies.

"Do they burn you?" I asked. "The fireflies?"

"Yes. If you can't make them stop, then they will. The flames are small, but there are a lot of them."

"The second trial is Waterfire," Mr Malkin said. "You'll walk through a pool full of stinging jellyfish. Their tentacles are very long and their fire will burn and paralyse you. If you can't make them retract their tentacles, then turn back. Their venom can kill you, if you get too much of it."

"Now don't scare the girl," Mrs Pommerans said, giving him a stern look.

144

"I'm not saying this to scare her. But she needs to know the truth. Surely living as Chimera's slave for a while is preferable to being dead?"

"I'm not sure about that," Shanaia said grimly. "Personally, I would rather die."

Kahla shot up from her seat. "Don't say that!" she hissed, pointing a gloved finger at Shanaia. "You mustn't ever say things like that!"

Shanaia looked a little stunned. I, too, was surprised. Was that Kahla leaping to my defence? It didn't seem like her. There had to be more to it.

Master Millaconda had stood up as well and he put his arm around Kahla.

"Hush, Kahla. Calm down." He wasn't telling her off, he was consoling her. Why? What did Kahla have to be upset about? Surely I was the one most in need of comfort right now?

"If I turn back, does that mean I've lost?" I said.

"Yes." Aunt Isa nodded. "That's the law."

I lost my temper.

"Law! What kind of law is that? I never asked to be a wildwitch and now I suddenly have to sit some lethal witch's exam – and if I don't pass, Chimera can do with me as she pleases. Do you call that justice?"

Aunt Isa stroked my hair.

"Poor Clara. It's hard, I know it is. The wildworld isn't a nice, easy place to live, for humans or animals. It's dangerous. Deadly, sometimes. And the laws of the wildwitches may resemble the laws of nature more closely than the ones you're used to. However, the strange thing is that justice, in some form or other, nearly always triumphs in the end."

"Not always," Shanaia said bitterly.

"No. Not always. But often. Trust in nature, Clara. And trust the wildwitch I know you have inside you."

As far as I knew, nature was a place where big animals ate small animals. Chimera was much bigger than me. I had no wish at all "to trust in nature".

"The third trial is Earthfire," Mr Malkin said. "That's where you walk through a cave where—"

"Stop it," I said. "Enough! I don't want to hear any more. It's not like I'm ever going to get through that... jellyfish pool."

"Clara..." Aunt Isa began.

"No. That's it. I'm going home!"

I stormed out and slammed the door behind me. The cat made it through just before it got its tail squished. It hissed angrily at me.

"Don't you start," I snapped at it. "This is all your fault, do you hear? If you'd left me alone then..."

Then none of this would have happened. I would still be Clara Ash from Year 7, a shy, ordinary girl with a few too many freckles, who lived with her mum in Jupiter Crescent and whose best friend was called Oscar.

Perhaps I should run away? Yes! Leave without telling anyone. Keep going until they stopped looking for me and then try to find my way home. Not using the wildways, I was too scared to use them, but even Raven Kettle had to be a place on a regular map, on the same planet as our flat and my school and the town I lived in. It might take me longer than travelling by the wildways, but sooner or later I'd come across normal people who would help me get home in the traditional way, by train or by bus or by plane, if necessary.

I ran across the circle towards Raven Kettle's entrance and the sunken road that led back to the forest. But before I got as far as that the cat blocked my path.

No, it said, inside my head.

"Go away," I said. "Move!"

But it stayed put, as big and immovable as on that very first rainy morning. It refused to let me pass.

Don't ever run before you have fought, it whispered. *Losing a fight means only that your opponent was stronger than you. But if you run without even trying...then your enemy is better than you. And then you'll never win anything again. Never ever.*

I had never heard the cat say so much before.

"You're just a cat," I said. "What would you know about that?"

Everything, it said. And then it moved out of my way so I could get past it, if that was what I wanted.

The choice was mine.

"That's not fair," I whispered. "Now I'll have to stay."

Because I knew it was right. If I left without even trying, then Chimera's victory would be complete. I would always know that I'd chickened out. That I was no good. That she and everybody else really were bigger and better and smarter than me, that I was a worthless loser.

I would rather die.

I hardly knew whether it was me or the cat who thought that, or both of us. But it was true.

The others sat together, looking at the door when I came back, as if they'd expected me. Kahla's eyes were big and as black as ink, and I could see that she'd been crying. But Aunt Isa smiled and gave me a little nod of approval.

"Right," I said. "Tell me about the last two trials."

CHAPTER 17

Skyfire

Torches flickered in the darkness and the moon hung large and pale above Raven Kettle. The ravens were now perched quietly in the trees, flapping their heavy wings only occasionally. The Raven Mothers stood on the ground below and there was a small crowd of spectators who had come to see how little Clara Ash would handle her trial by wildfire. Only Kahla hadn't been allowed to watch. This time she had argued and protested so long that her dad had eventually pulled her to one side and spoken to her through clenched teeth.

I wondered why it was so important for her to be here. She who hated the cold. Was it to support me or was it simply because she didn't want to miss seeing me fail?

Chimera was standing a short distance away,

so close that her wings would touch me if she unfurled them.

"I hope you're ready, witch child," she whispered icily. "Too late to run away now..."

I glanced furtively at her. Did she know... did she understand how close I'd come to doing just that? I could see from her triumphant look that she didn't expect me to succeed.

I hoped she was wrong, but I had a horrible feeling that she might be right.

"Let the trial commence," Thuja announced.

The night sky filled with tiny, glowing dots. They whirled around us in an amazing aerial display like living fireworks.

"Oh!" I couldn't help exclaiming. I hadn't expected it to be beautiful.

One of the fire dots hovered briefly in front of my nose, so I could see its delicate wings and its large, blinking and golden body. Then it was gone. But one of the others had touched my hand.

"Ouch!" I just about managed to suppress the outburst and Chimera smiled scornfully. She caught one of the blinking fireflies in her hand and held it, just to show me that she could. I heard it hum and buzz inside her taloned fist. Then she let it go again.

My own hand still stung. The pain was mild, but then again there had only been one firefly. What would happen if they all settled on me? There were thousands, possibly millions of them.

All seven Raven Mothers started to hum and the fireflies instantly stopped their dance and started to fly in circles so that their fire created a kind of whirling tunnel in the air.

"Am I meant to go through this?" I asked.

"Yes," Aunt Isa said. "Let them see you. Let them come to you. If you let them come close and you're not lying, they won't burn you."

It was easier said than done. I knew now how much it hurt when just a single firefly burned me. I reminded myself that the fireflies were the easiest trial. It would get much worse after this one.

I took a step towards the firefly tunnel. I had a strong urge to race through it as fast as I could, but I knew that wouldn't be a good idea. Mrs Pommerans's advice had been: "Give them time to get to know you."

I stepped in among the dancing fireflies. There were so many of them that all I could see was their light. Raven Kettle disappeared. Chimera, the Raven Mothers, Aunt Isa and everyone else... they were all gone now and only the fireflies and I were left behind. And one other being.

Stand still, the cat whispered silently in my mind.

It was with me. I couldn't see it, it must be creeping around in the darkness outside the circle, but it was in my head and I wasn't alone.

I stood still. It was hotter here than outside the tunnel, much hotter. I started to sweat. But although the fireflies flew past me and circled my face, my hair and my hands, they didn't land on me. And neither did they burn me.

They didn't burn me...

"I'm not lying," I said in a low and cautious voice. "Chimera is the liar."

I don't know if they understood me. But at one stroke they were gone. The tunnel dissolved and the fireflies took one last, wild swoop across the circle before they disappeared.

I caught sight of Chimera's face again. Expressionless. Possibly no longer quite so sure that I would fail?

"Clara Ash has passed Skyfire," Thuja said, and I told myself that there was a hint of satisfaction in her voice.

Valla sighed.

"Oh well," he said. "Then I suppose we'll all have to plod down to the jellyfish pool. And in this weather..."

CHAPTER 18

Waterfire

The ravens followed us. Squawking, they flitted past us in the moonlight like shadows, landed on trees and waited for us to catch up before taking off and flying on again. They quite clearly knew where we were going.

Because of my bad knee I was allowed to ride on Star even though I think it was against the rules. Everyone else was walking, even Mrs Pommerans. The forest around us was so big and dark that our torches and lanterns looked like tiny fireflies. I shuddered, and suddenly thought I could hear something rustle in the thicket behind us. A fox, maybe, or a bigger animal? I wondered if there were wolves in a place like this.

Then it struck me that a wolf or two would be nothing compared to what awaited me, and I stopped looking over my shoulder.

The jellyfish pool lay in a valley surrounded by snow-topped rocks. There was, however, no snow near the pool and the dark water was steaming slightly.

"How deep is it?" I asked Mr Malkin, who was walking on one side of Star. "I won't drown, will I?"

"No," he said. "Not if you stay on your feet. I think the water will come up to your chest at its deepest point."

Chimera was there, too, of course. Her wings cast blue shadows across the snow in front of us.

"You know this can kill you, don't you?" she said. "They say people scream for hours while they try to scratch off their own skin. And then they die. Why don't you just admit that you lied? Then you won't have to endure that kind of pain."

Mr Malkin turned around.

"Be quiet, Chimera," he said. "The law doesn't allow you to threaten and intimidate a witness."

But it was too late. The words had been spoken and I couldn't get them out of my head.

Star carefully descended the last stretch of the slope, which was clear of snow, and stopped. I patted her and thanked her for the ride, sincerely hoping that it wouldn't be the last time I sat on her round back.

I was supposed to take off almost all my clothes. My fingers were shaking so badly that Aunt Isa had to help me with the buttons on my raincoat and again I heard a snort of derision from Chimera.

"The girl's terrified," she announced. "Let's put an end to this ridiculous performance so we can all go home."

No one responded. But Aunt Isa kissed my cheek and whispered into my ear. "Trust in nature – and in yourself. They won't hurt you."

Thuja and the other Raven Mothers formed a circle around the rock pool and again started humming monotonously, as they had done with the fireflies. Something in the water began to glow. It was the jellyfish. I could see them now. And they weren't the clear little blobs of jelly I'd imagined. They looked like large, transparent church bells floating through the water, their tentacles as long, fat and knobbly as those of an octopus.

"Let the trial commence," Thuja said.

Steps had been carved into the rock and I was supposed to walk down them. As I stepped onto the first one, I was shaking all over and couldn't feel my legs at all. They won't hurt you, I kept whispering to myself, but it was hard to believe it, and when the water touched my ankles at the first step, I stopped. It was warm. Not as warm as bathwater, but after the cold, frosty air it almost felt like it.

I looked up. Chimera was standing at the edge of the pool, right behind two of the Raven Mothers. Her yellow eyes met mine.

"They scream for hours," she said in a low voice, just loud enough for me to hear.

Now that ought to have terrified me even more. But it didn't. I think I was already as scared as a human being could get. And it was then that I realized she didn't want me to go into the water. That was the reason she was intimidating me, the reason she was trying to frighten me into giving up.

She thinks I can do it.

The thought came out of the blue, or rather, out of her menacing, yellow gaze: if she was so sure that I didn't stand a chance, why was she trying so hard to make me give up?

How strange that Chimera apparently had more faith in me than I did.

This realization made me walk down the next steps, deeper into the water.

I waited for the pain, but it didn't come.

The jellyfish floated around me and one of them softly bumped against my leg, a strange rubbery sensation. But they didn't sting me. Aunt Isa was right. I could trust nature – and possibly myself a little bit.

Slowly I waded across the pool and out the other side.

I got soaked, but that was all.

"Clara Ash has passed Waterfire," Thuja announced.

"Y ou're halfway," Aunt Isa said while she dried my shoulders with a towel. "And you've done brilliantly. Here, put this jumper on before you freeze to death."

I pulled the jumper over my head with shaking arms. And this time it was because I was cold. Winter bathing was definitely not a sport I would ever want to take up.

I felt very odd. Almost as if I could never be scared again. Or at least, not *as* scared. At long last I felt just as big on the inside as everybody else. It was wonderful.

"They didn't hurt me," I said, probably for the fifth time. "They actually didn't hurt me."

"No," Aunt Isa said and smiled. "I told you so."

CHAPTER 19

Earthfire

I was only halfway, but it felt like more than that. And the thought of the third trial, Earthfire, frightened me much less than the stinging jellyfish.

I would have to walk through a cave. Fire lizards that looked like small dragons lived inside it, Mrs Pommerans had explained. They would spew clouds of flaming gas into the air and that might be uncomfortable, obviously, but in my opinion not as bad as the venomous tentacles of the jellyfish. And since the jellyfish hadn't hurt me, why would the fire lizards be more hostile?

Chimera glared at me and I thought I could already see defeat in her scowl.

Just you wait, I thought to myself. You'll be the loser and I'll win this trial. Because I really *am* a wildwitch. I might not be the best wildwitch in the world, but I wasn't lying. They'll let me pass.

I actually believed it.

The entrance to the cave was a hole in the ground, not much bigger than one of the basement windows at home.

"This time you'll be on your own," Mrs Pommerans said. "We won't be able to see you until you come out on the other side. And this trial is a little harder because it's not enough that the fire lizards don't hurt you, they also have to help you. Their fire is your only light down there and, without that, it'll be difficult for you to find your way out."

"Yes," I said. "I understand."

"In that case, there's nothing more I can tell you, little witch. Good luck."

No one was humming this time. Was that because I had to rouse the fire lizards myself, if I wanted their help? I couldn't help feeling a little cheated. All the wildwitches did was tie a rope around my waist and lower me into a hole, and it felt rather unceremonious. It was nowhere near as stylish as the first two trials.

But then again it isn't about style, I told myself. It's about survival and proving that Chimera is lying and not me!

As I'd expected, it was dark inside the cave. Dark and damp as in a basement. I landed awkwardly and felt a twinge in my knee – not a sharp pain, just a gentle warning that I couldn't be sure how long it would support me.

I wondered how far it was to the exit. No one had told me anything about that. What if I couldn't walk that far?

I untied myself from the rope they'd lowered me down with. It disappeared up into the air and soon afterwards a cover was pushed across the opening so that the last remnant of moon and torchlight disappeared.

Now it was properly dark. Pitch black.

And that was when I got scared.

I realized that I hadn't thought this trial through. How would I make the fire lizards light up the cave? I guess I'd imagined that I could fumble my way to the exit without any light if they couldn't be bothered to help. But as soon as I took my first, tentative step, I knew that wouldn't work. I stubbed my toe on something hard, I stumbled and only avoided falling because I bumped into the rough wall of the cave and was able to hold onto it.

I couldn't risk a fall. I could break both arms and legs, even my neck, and my knee wouldn't tolerate many more knocks on top of the ones it had already got.

"Eh... lizards?" I began cautiously, trying not to feel too silly. "Are you there?"

Of course there was no reply. Did I hear a faint scurrying in the darkness? I wasn't sure. Besides, I didn't know what a lizard sounded like when it moved.

"This is stupid," I mumbled to myself. And this time I thought I could hear a faint echo whisper *stupid-stupid-stupid* after I had stopped talking.

I bit my lip. Now what? Simply shouting **GOAWAY** wouldn't get me anywhere, and that was the only witchery I knew.

Perhaps it's time for you to learn something new.

I hesitated.

"Cat? Is that you?"

But the cat didn't reply either. Perhaps that hadn't even been it. I couldn't always tell whether the voice belonged to the cat or to me.

Closing my eyes when it was already so black that I couldn't see a thing seemed pointless, but

I did it anyway. This was how Aunt Isa had first taught me to find my wildsense and it was still easier this way.

If you could call it easy.

See nothing, hear nothing, smell nothing.

Connect with this other sense that had nothing to do with the eyes, ears or nose. The one that could hear every living creature in the whole wildworld – including the creatures hiding in the darkness of the cave.

There.

Very close to me, in fact. So close that I would have tripped over one if I'd taken another step. A small, cool spark of life flickered in the darkness, a tiny heart beat slowly and coldly.

The poor thing is cold, I thought, and I immediately wanted to pick it up and hold it in my hands so I could share my own warmth with it.

Hsssssssssss...

A flame shot out between us, so bright that I could sense it through my closed eyelids. I opened my eyes. For a moment a glowing cloud hung between me and the lizard and I could see it. It was yellow with black spots, its scaly body was warty and spiny and its eyes bulged as if there weren't enough room for them in its broad, toady head. It wasn't very big, either – maybe the size

of a guinea pig or a kitten, but a lot less cute.
I had time to see it take a few waddling steps
towards me before the gas cloud dispersed and
the light faded away. Soon I felt its claws against
my trouser leg.

Heat. I knew that was why it was attracted to
me. It had sensed my wish to share my body heat,
and now I was stuck with it. After all, I had made
a kind of promise.

All right. Nobody is saying you have to kiss
it, I thought. Just hold it for a little while. I bent
down and carefully lifted up the rough and gnarly
animal and held it close to my heart. It wasn't
actually that difficult, although the lizard certainly
wasn't soft, warm or furry. It was a bit like stroking

coarse sandpaper with prickles on it, but I could feel that the lizard enjoyed it and needed all the heat I could give it. After a few minutes it even started grunting with pleasure and contentment, and the sound became a throaty hum strangely like the Raven Mothers' wildsong.

Hissssssssss. Hisssssssss. Hissssssssss.

Suddenly the whole cave was ablaze with light. On the walls, on the ceiling, along the floor, anywhere there was even the slightest protruding rock or a hint of a hollow... the fire lizards were everywhere and they breathed their glowing clouds into the air as if they were singing in a choir. A fire song, golden, warm and red, lighting up the dark.

I held "my" lizard close and I nearly cried because it was so beautiful. Just as beautiful as the dance of the fireflies – or possibly even more so because I understood it better. They liked the warmth. They liked me. They sang their fire song because they were happy.

"Thank you," I whispered as I slowly stroked the lizard's neck with my index finger. It arched its neck and pushed against my touch, making it a little firmer, and hummed even louder. Still holding the little lizard, I started to walk.

It wasn't very far. One hundred paces, perhaps, if it had been a straight path, but it wasn't. I had to climb and crawl and squeeze myself through the narrowest of places and everywhere sharp rocks shot up from the floor or hung down from the ceiling. Hidden among the rock spikes were cracks and chasms, some so deep and wide that a twelve-year-old girl could have easily disappeared into them. Without the light from the lizards I would never have found my way out.

The exit from the cave was somewhat bigger than the entrance, a jagged hole in the roof seven or eight metres above me. A rope ladder hung down from two solid beams and I could see the torches and the moonlight outside and hear voices even though I couldn't make out what they were saying.

I put the fire lizard down on a small rock and stroked its neck one last time.

"I'll come back one day," I promised it, "... and warm you up again."

There were fewer gas clouds now and they glowed for shorter intervals. "My" lizard burped a final, golden fire greeting into the air. Then it crawled down from the rock and disappeared into the darkness. I grabbed hold of the rope ladder and started my climb towards the moonlight. My knee hurt and I didn't like the way the rope creaked, but I would be up and out in a few seconds and then I would have passed the third trial.

Or so I thought.

When I reached for the next rung of the rope ladder, my hand didn't touch rope. Instead it closed around something cold and furry. A piercing screech rang out and a set of very sharp teeth sank into my finger.

Suddenly the darkness of the cave came alive with claws and teeth and flapping and screaming. Leathery wings hit my face and the back of my neck, I couldn't breathe, there were furry bodies everywhere scratching and biting and shrieking in a high-pitched tone that drilled into my ears and all the way to my brain. My heart pounded and I lost my grip on the rope ladder. I slipped and fell; my leg got caught in one of the rungs and I briefly hung upside down before I crashed onto the stony and uneven cave floor below.

Nothing.

All the creatures went away.

Darkness.

Pain.

A tingling sensation of wings and claws all over me.

Then that, too, disappeared and I no longer knew where I was.

CHAPTER 20

A Friend in Need

"Clara!"

Someone was shaking me.

"Clara, come on! Sit up."

I had no desire to sit up. I had no wish to move at all. Everything hurt and my stupid knee had found new and interesting ways to torture me – a fiery dart, a prickling of acid, needles pushing in behind the kneecap and sending electric shocks up through my thigh muscle.

"Clara. You have to!"

It was Kahla.

Kahla? What was she doing here?

"What..." I mumbled. "Why are..."

But I couldn't finish my sentences. The words slipped away when I reached for them and my tongue felt numb. All that came out were grunts of pain.

"Where does it hurt?" Kahla asked.

"Knee. Head."

She placed her hands either side of my head. I noticed in my dazed state that she was still wearing mittens. But what was she doing to me?

"Lie still. I'll see if I can make it go away."

And then she did pretty much the same as Aunt Isa had done that first night. She stroked my temples and the back of my head with woolly mitten fingers while her wildsong curled around me as subtly as my black cat. It helped. Perhaps not as much as when Aunt Isa did it, but it did help. I could think again, I could move again.

"What are you doing here?" I asked.

"Helping you," she said through gritted teeth. "What did you expect? That you could manage everything on your own?"

"Yes," I said. "Aren't those the rules?"

"Chimera doesn't play by the rules. It might explain why she always wins."

"Chimera?" I looked around frantically. There was a torch lying next to Kahla and it cast strange shadows between the rocks. I caught a glimpse of curious lizard eyes, but I couldn't see a four-metre-tall non-angel.

"Don't worry. She's up there waiting with the others."

"Then how can she be mixed up in this..."

Kahla scoffed. "Perhaps you think it was just bad luck that a colony of bats decided to attack you just as you were about to pass the third trial?"

Bats. Yes. That was why I had fallen.

"But..."

"Clara. Bats are shy. They would never attack a human – unless someone made them."

I reached for the torch and swept the beam across the roof of the cave. There they hung, the bats – in furry clusters, heads down, their wings folded around their bodies. They hardly stirred now; they swayed a little and occasionally there was the soft rustling of a wing. I thought they still looked fairly scary, but I had to admit that they showed no sign of wanting to attack us. Perhaps I'd just seen too many vampire movies.

I shuddered.

"How do you know that's what happened?" I asked.

"Because I followed you. As soon as the grown-ups had moved away from the hole you were lowered into, I climbed down as well."

"Why? I didn't think... I mean, I didn't think you liked me."

Kahla looked away.

169

"I don't. Or... it's a bit difficult to explain. It's... it's incredibly important that I become a good wildwitch. Far more important than you can imagine. Isa is supposed to teach me all the things my dad can't because he's a man. That's why we come to see her, day in, day out, even though it's a terribly long way to travel and it's dreadfully cold and I freeze half to death every single day. Because it's *important*." She glanced up at me. Her dark eyes shone as if she were about to cry. "And then you came. And you knew nothing. Isa had to tell you everything, even the basics, and you still couldn't do it. You would cheat or guess at most of the answers, and sulk when you didn't get things right straight away. Suddenly I had to wait for the new girl to catch up all the time, and to top it all you couldn't even be bothered to make an effort. When I've been practising my entire life. You've no idea how angry it made me."

I squirmed. She was right: I'd sulked and been stroppy at the beginning, and I'd cheated in some of the tasks because I didn't understand them.

"Why is it so important to you?" I asked. "Becoming a good wildwitch, I mean."

Again she avoided looking at me.

"I want to be just as good as my mum was," she said quietly. "It's absolutely essential."

"Your mum?"

She lifted her head abruptly.

"Stop asking so many questions," she snapped.

"You hated me right from the start," I said.

She shrugged her shoulders. "Yes. Or rather hated that you were there. After all, I didn't know you."

"Then why are you helping me now?"

She snorted.

"I hadn't planned to. I decided to follow you to see if you cheated."

That made more sense. Now I recognized her.

"I didn't."

"No," she said. "But Chimera did. So it was probably just as well that I was here, don't you think?"

I sighed.

"Yes," I said. "I guess so."

"And now you have to climb up that rope ladder and show them that you really are a wildwitch. You understand Chimera has to be beaten, don't you?"

"What about you?"

"I'll go back to the entrance and get out that way. It's probably best that they don't find out I helped you. Even though Chimera cheated first."

I did as she told me. I heard her clamber over
the rocks in the darkness while I stretched out
my battered body and prepared to limp back to
the rope ladder. Kahla. She was a bit like the cat.
I didn't think that we'd just become best friends
forever, but she'd helped me when I needed it and
I knew that I owed her a favour. Perhaps that was
a kind of friendship.

When I struggled up the last few rungs of
the rope ladder, all the grown-ups were waiting – friends, enemies and Raven Mothers. Aunt
Isa smiled and I could see an extra sparkle in her
brown eyes. Chimera's scowl was more evil than
ever. And there was a look on her face which made
me fairly sure that Kahla had been right – she
really had tried to stop me with the bats. But she'd
failed, I thought. Kahla had seen to that.

"Clara Ash has passed Earthfire," Thuja said
out loud so that everyone could hear it.

Only one trial remained – the one Mrs Pommerans had called the Heartfire.

CHAPTER 21

Heartfire

"It has been a long time since we last saw a wildwitch undergo this fourth and final trial," Thuja said. "This is the most dangerous one for Clara, but it also carries a certain risk for the rest of us. Therefore I now ask both parties if they still maintain their allegations. Clara, is there anything in your testimony you wish to change?"

I shook my head.

"Everything I said is true," I said. My voice sounded slightly croaky, but otherwise loud and clear and very calm. Was that really me? I hardly recognized myself.

Thuja faced Chimera, who was standing next to me in the circle of trees in Raven Kettle. She was so close that I could have touched her wing if I'd stretched out my hand. I didn't.

"Chimera, Clara stands by her testimony. What is your answer?"

"That she's lying." There was no hesitation in Chimera's voice either, but something had changed. She wasn't quite as arrogant as she'd been at the start, back when she thought I was a bug she could easily squash.

"You know that if Clara walks through the fire unhurt and comes out on the other side then she has proved her case?"

"So you say."

"Listen, Chimera," Valla suddenly intervened. "She passed the first three trials. No one here seriously doubts that she's telling the truth."

Wow! Was this the same Valla who'd been so crotchety with me at the start? He'd certainly changed his tune. Or perhaps he just wanted the case over and done with. It must be nearly midnight now, possibly even later. And he was the one who'd been the least enthusiastic about walking all the way to the jellyfish pool and the lizard cave.

"Will you deny me my right, Valla Raven?"

He grunted. "No, but your sentence will be less harsh if you don't endanger us all by persisting. Can't we end it here?"

"Are you scared, Valla?" The contempt in

Chimera's voice was as sharp as a knife. "Then give me the girl and go home to bed. If you give her to me now, I'm willing to release her after only one year."

One year! Twelve months. Three hundred and sixty-five days. Eight thousand seven hundred and sixty hours. No thanks. No way.

"It appears we'll have to continue," Thuja said. "Very well. So be it."

I was told to stand exactly at the centre of the circle of trees. Everyone else – including Chimera – had to withdraw to the far side of Raven Kettle, beyond the trees. I wondered if Kahla was hiding somewhere out there and watching what was happening. I thought so, even though I couldn't see her.

The seven Raven Mothers took up position by the trees that made up the circle.

They started singing.

This time it was more than a quiet hum. They were still singing without words, but so loudly that I wanted to cover my ears with my hands. It was as if the trees, the earth and the air quivered. The sound grew louder and louder until it was almost unbearable.

The snow melted. Not slowly and gradually, but within seconds, like a knob of butter on a red-hot frying pan. Under my feet the earth stirred restlessly and then started to crack. Lines of fire raced across the ground from each of the seven Raven Mothers towards me. Just before the lines of fire reached me, they diverted to form a ring, a wall of flames that burned so hot and hungry that I was forced to close my eyes. I felt my eyelashes and eyebrows crumble and turn to ashes.

I was standing at the heart of a fire star. And I wasn't alone.

There was something else inside the fire. I couldn't see it, I was too scared to open my eyes, but I could feel it with my wildsense. The fire was alive. It wasn't just something, it was *someone*.

Who are you?

It was the fire asking the question, not me. The roaring, all-consuming fire that could swallow me up in one single breath, burn me to a crisp and reduce me to bones and ashes.

It wasn't just asking for my name. It wanted to know who I was.

"A wildwitch," I whispered, trying not to inhale too much of the boiling hot air into my lungs. "I'm a wildwitch."

And what is that?

I panicked for a moment. How would I explain that? Was there even a right answer? Or a wrong one?

"Someone who loves animals. Someone who loves the whole wildworld."

It wasn't wrong, I could feel it. But the fire's heart was still waiting. There would seem to be more.

Something Aunt Isa had once said suddenly mingled with the memory of the happy song of the fire lizards.

"Someone who never takes without giving..." I began.

The flames retreated noticeably. It didn't get much cooler, but at least it no longer felt like a thousand sunburns. But it still wasn't enough. I was missing something.

The cat. The cat was a part of it now, a part of me.

"Someone who doesn't flee without having fought first."

You have fought, little wildwitch. But did you do it alone?

Oh no.

The fear sent a shiver down my spine and set my heart racing. I couldn't breathe and the flames closed in on me again. It felt as if my skin were seconds from bubbling up like pork crackling under the grill, and I knew why.

Because I hadn't fought alone. Kahla had helped me. Only because Chimera had cheated, but even so.

Lie, I thought. Say that you were alone. After all, nobody saw her...

But I couldn't. I couldn't lie to the fire. It would either have to take me or leave me alone; I had to speak the truth.

"No," I croaked. "A friend... helped me."

You'll be burned alive, I thought. Because you cheated. The fire will take you and reduce you to ashes.

But it didn't. Instead it asked me quietly, once more, and it was as if there were an undercurrent of laughter in its voice:

Who are you, little wildwitch?

And then I understood. It was why we were here. It was what the trial was all about.

"Someone who speaks the truth," I said. "Someone who speaks the truth – or stays silent."

There could be no doubt now. The flames were laughing, they danced around me, wild and affectionate at the same time, but they didn't hurt me. Their roar turned into a song, red and golden in the darkness of the night. And when I finally dared open my eyes, that was when I saw it.

The firebird.

With feathers and wings of flames, its neck, tail and beak made from fire, its eyes like liquid gold. It rose towards the sky in a burst of sparks that scattered over me like stars from a sparkler.

Well answered, little wildwitch. You have the fire in your heart.

It swept across the treetops and made the ravens flap their wings, it swooped down on me in a loving and teasing dance before rising again, soaring and soaring until it was just a flame-coloured silhouette against the moon.

Then it was gone. And the silence was total.

Of the seven Raven Mothers only one was still standing: Thuja. Her voice was croakier than her raven's; she was swaying and had to support herself against the tree behind her.

"Clara Ash has passed the Heartfire," she said. And then she slumped down with her back against her tree.

I didn't feel tired at all. Not yet. It was as if the firebird's laughter were still bubbling inside me, and not even my knee hurt now.

"You did it!" cheered Kahla, who was the first to reach me. She grabbed both my arms and danced around with me until everything in front of my eyelash-less eyes started to spin. "You did it, you did it, you did it!"

"Oh, my dear," Aunt Isa said. "Your old aunt is so proud of you."

And a large cat, as black as midnight, strolled towards us, purring like a well-oiled motorbike.

Mine, it sang contentedly and proudly inside my head. *My wildwitch.*

But our celebrations were short-lived. The ravens, the crows, the jackdaws and all the rooks started squawking and screaming and hissing at once. In unison they took flight and ascended towards the moon like a black cloud.

"Now what?" I said, stunned. "What's happening?"

Thuja grabbed the bark on the tree trunk and got back on her feet.

"It's Chimera," she said. "She has fled."

And then I saw her, a larger shape in-between the others, a giant bird who wasn't a bird and most certainly not an angel, either. The ravens chased her, but her huge eagle wings weren't just for show, and the black birds started dropping like stones, feathered black balls falling and crashing to the ground.

"No!" Thuja cried out in despair, pressing both hands against her blind eyes. "The ravens are dying! She's killing the ravens!"

I don't think I'll ever forget the look on her

face. Her blind grief wasn't just for the sight she no longer had. She scrambled around on her hands and knees, touching one dead bird after another, but she couldn't find the raven that had once been hers.

CHAPTER 22

The Last Word

Nearly half the great black birds in Raven Kettle died that night. And Chimera escaped. She was declared an outlaw and shunned by the wildworld, but although the survivors looked for her for as long as their necks or wings could carry them, they never found her. It was as if the ground had swallowed her up – or perhaps, more accurately, as if she'd been spirited away into the dark midnight air.

Thuja sat by the fireplace in her room where she could feel the warmth against her face although she could no longer see the flames. Her hands lay empty and idle in her lap.

"I'm sorry," I said. "I wish there was something I could do."

Thuja turned at the sound of my voice, but she didn't get up.

"It's not your fault," she said. "We only have ourselves to blame."

"Why?"

"We should have listened sooner. And we should have made new laws a long time ago so we wouldn't have been forced to try you as they did in the days of Bravita Bloodling." She held out both her hands and after a moment's confusion I realized that she wanted to say goodbye. I put my hand in hers. Although her grip was warm and light, I could feel how much strength there was in her still. "It's time for you to go home now, Clara Ash. I promise you that we'll keep looking for Chimera. She won't be allowed to hurt you again. But I rather think that black cat of yours would stop her if she tried, don't you?"

"I think so," I said, and couldn't help smiling. "And perhaps a couple of other friends, too. But what about you? Will you... will you ever be able to see again?"

"In time," she said. "When the new brood is hatched in spring I'll start over with a new chick. It usually takes a year or two before you get to know each other well enough to borrow one another's senses."

"Good luck," I said, and meant it.

"You too, Clara Ash."

When we emerged from the fog of the wild-ways at the gate by the white stones, the first thing I saw was the little blue Kia parked in the yard next to Aunt Isa's rusty old banger.

"Mum!"

I barely had to touch Star with my heels, she was that keen to return to her safe, warm stable. We ended up galloping down the gravel road with clumps of grass flying around our ears until we reached the farmhouse.

The door opened and Mum and Bumble came out. Bumble behaved as he always did – bouncing and dancing and wagging his tail and getting in his own way and almost under Star's hooves, too. Mum stood still, as if she could barely believe her own eyes.

"Clara Mouse! Oh, sweetheart..."

I let myself slide down from Star's back and dropped the reins so the horse could wander back to the stable. No new stable door had been fitted, so the goats were free to come and go as they pleased.

"You sounded so strange on the phone," Mum said, pulling me close and hugging me in a way she hadn't done since I was eight. "So I had to come. And when you weren't here..." She gulped

down a big mouthful of air and hugged me even tighter. "You were gone such a long time. I didn't know what to think..."

"But now we're back," I said. "And tomorrow we can go home together!"

But that wasn't the end of the story, obviously. I had to tell Oscar what had happened and make Cat understand that it wasn't cool to sink four sharp cat claws into the soft nose of Oscar's labrador. Oscar was the only one I told because we tell each other everything. Everyone else just thought I'd been ill and away at some kind of home for sick children to recover. I also had to persuade Aunt Isa to buy a mobile and walk up the hill to call us every now and then with news of Bumble, Star, the goats and all the other animals. And of Kahla.

"You won't be held back by the new girl now," I told her when we said goodbye.

"No," she said. "So I'll probably learn more." But then she gave me a quick woolly hug. "Take care of yourself. And... if you did come back, I wouldn't actually mind..."

It felt weird to be back in the flat and with Oscar and at school again. I'd been gone almost three weeks. Twenty days when I counted them.

It felt more like twenty months. Everything felt so different, especially on the inside.

"My," Mum said the first morning I was going back to school, "haven't you grown?"

"Yes," I said. "I think I have."

That's because you have me.

I looked down and met Cat's amber eyes. He looked incredibly pleased with himself.

"I think I can manage growing without your help," I huffed.

He snorted. *I don't think so.*

There was no point in arguing. When you have a cat, don't ever expect to get the last word.

NEXT IN THE WILDWITCH SERIES

PUSHKIN CHILDREN'S BOOKS

Just as we all are, children are fascinated by stories. From the earliest age, we love to hear about monsters and heroes, romance and death, disaster and rescue, from every place and time.

We created Pushkin Children's Books to share these tales from different languages and cultures with younger readers, and to open the door to the wide, colourful worlds these stories offer.

From picture books and adventure stories to fairy tales and classics, and from fifty-year-old bestsellers to current huge successes abroad, the books on the Pushkin Children's list reflect the very best stories from around the world, for our most discerning readers of all: children.